OH'DAR'S QUEST

WRAK-AYYA: THE AGE OF SHADOWS BOOK THREE

LEIGH ROBERTS

DRAGON WINGS PRESS

CONTENTS

Editing by Joy Sephton http://www.justemagine.biz
Cover design by Cherie Fox http://www.cheriefox.com

Sexual activities or events in this book are intended for adults.

ISBN: 978-1-951528-00-3 (ebook)
ISBN: 978-1-951528-13-3 (paperback)

Dedication

For everyone who still wonders, still dreams, still asks...

What If?

CHAPTER 1

I n the Great Chamber, Adia, Healer of the People of the High Rocks, sat across the table from Acaraho, their High Protector, enjoying a brief moment of rest. The giant hall was relatively empty. It was midday, and the unpaired bachelors who gathered for breakfast had already cleared out. Despite the warmer temperatures starting to build outside, the rock interior of Kthama was pleasantly cool.

The Great Entrance, the Great Chamber, and many of the living quarters were situated on the first level of the underground cave system. Tunnels led to the lower levels where other dedicated living spaces and communal living areas were located. Empty rooms of various sizes were scattered throughout all the levels, used for meetings, special activities, or storage as needed. The Mother Stream that brought the lifeblood of oxygen and nutrients ran through the lowest level.

"The offspring have finished marking off where we will plant the crops in the garden areas that the males prepared," shared Adia.

All the offspring were excited to help the Healer; after all, she was Second Rank. And they enjoyed being around Adia; her gentle nature and kind eyes put them at ease.

"I watched them interacting with you for a while. The older ones seemed interested in learning about what was being planted," replied Acaraho.

"Yes, but the little ones always only want to play with the colored seeds," she laughed. Then she added, more seriously, "There is still not one who stands out as a candidate."

Healers often found their successor in working with the offspring. Often there was one particular young female who would catch on a little quicker, make intuitive leaps in understanding, already have the answer to the next question before it had been asked. These were indicators of the higher seventh sense with which Healers were born. And though all the offspring were bright and precious, that special one had not yet surfaced. Adia preferred to have the next Healer come from within the People of the High Rocks rather than from another community.

I am still young, but no one lives forever.

Acaraho interrupted her thoughts. "You told me your talents became evident when you were very young, and I know you are hoping one of our own will surface. I well remember the day you came to the High Rocks; your father passed not long after."

"Yes," she replied softly. "The day my father told me I was to be the Healer of the High Rocks, I thought my heart would break in two. I did not want to leave Awenasa. I knew it was an honor to be selected, but Awenasa was my home. However, the High Council had decided, and that was the end of it."

Had Adia been male, she would have inherited her father's position of leadership. Instead, when her father passed, his brother took over as Leader of the People of the Deep Valley. It grieved Adia deeply that she had not been there when her father returned to the Great Spirit. She knew he would never have wanted her to feel this way, but she felt she had let him down—that perhaps she might have been able to save him.

They fell silent for a moment, then Adia looked up to see her son, Nootau, approaching with Nadi-wani, the Healer's Helper. Nootau came up close to his mother, and she put an arm around him and hugged him. He hugged her in return.

Though he still had filling out to do, it was apparent that he was going to have his father's build. His father, the great Khon'Tor, Leader of the People, who had, Without Her Consent, mated with and seeded Adia.

Since then, Adia had found a pace with Khon'Tor

that worked between them. There was still tension, and Adia would never forget how he had attacked her, but out of her sense of responsibility as Healer, she had kept Khon'Tor's horrendous secret. She believed that no one could take his place if she were to hold him to account.

Acaraho could, in theory, have filled the position of Leader—he had everything Khon'Tor did, except the overarching drive to be in command. But the next Leader had to come from Khon'Tor's bloodline.

All the commotion of the earlier times had now settled down, and the last few years had been uneventful.

Adia thought back to the conversation she'd had with Acaraho the night before.

"The truth has a way of coming out," she had said anxiously. *"The bigger Nootau gets, the more he looks like his father. And if, as he matures, Nootau develops the same white streak on his head that Khon'Tor has, then all the effort of keeping his parentage a secret will be for nothing."*

There was no mistaking Khon'Tor, the Leader of the People of the High Rocks, with that startling silver crest. Combined with his other attributes, it gave him a striking appearance. But for now, only she, Acaraho, and three others knew that Khon'Tor was the father of Nootau, and they would all keep their silence.

All the males of the People were tall and well-built, but only two were as magnificent as Khon'Tor and Acaraho. Though Adia and Acaraho were not aware of the extent of the gossip, the People assumed that it was Acaraho who had seeded Nootau. The close relationship between Adia and Acaraho was no secret, though they strived not to show affection for each other in public. But, considering their strong ties, and that he had stepped up to be the male role model for her two offspring—Oh'Dar, the adopted White child, and Nootau—it was a natural jump to the wrong conclusion.

"I am so grateful to you, Acaraho, for persuading the High Council to allow me to keep Nootau. And I believe your promise to mentor both Nootau and Oh'Dar made the final difference in the Overseer's view."

Adia's thoughts now turned to her eldest son. She had noticed Oh'Dar going through bouts of melancholy. It was not like him, and it bothered her more than she admitted.

I must talk to Acaraho about it again later when we next have some private time together.

While Adia and Acaraho were talking, Khon'Tor was in his living quarters pondering the matter of pairing. It had been many years since his mate, Hakani, stepped off the edge of the grassy path to fall to her death in the churning waters far below. By all means, he should have selected another mate by now. He was obligated as Leader to be paired and produce offspring.

If Khon'Tor ever considered that Nootau had a right to the leadership, he never let it bother him. He had put the boy out of his mind from the beginning. His only regret, if Khon'Tor had regrets, was that Hakani had claimed to be seeded by him at last, and took his unborn offspring with her when she had stepped off the ledge.

The other females of the community had stepped up to fill much of Hakani's role in his life. He did not want for meals, or housekeeping, or any of the mechanics that needed to take place around the Leader's Quarters. And lots of females would be honored to be paired with the Leader of the largest Sasquatch community known in their region.

There were still many years in which he could father offspring, but there was more to pairing than that.

Hakani's last words haunted him, taunting him with fear of exposure by his next mate—one over whom he would not have the hold he had over her.

His next mate might not keep quiet about his taste for mating Without Her Consent, which broke the People's First Law. Khon'Tor had taken his satisfaction with Hakani by frightening and intimidating her. The more she fought him, and the more he could dominate her, the more exquisitely pleasurable it was for him.

Time was passing, but though Khon'Tor knew he

needed to take a mate, he just did not know how to create enough leverage to force her silence about his sadistic tastes.

In the Brothers' village, Oh'Dar sat in front of the fire outside the dwelling of Is'Taqa, Second Chief of the Brothers. He poked at the flames with a long stick, head down, lost in thought, only occasionally looking up at the others. The crackling fire reflected in his blue eyes that were often smiling but were somber tonight. He loved to spend time with Is'Taqa, who had become like an uncle to him. Just as Acaraho was teaching Oh'Dar the People's skills, so Is'Taqa was teaching him those of the Brothers.

Is'Taqa and Honovi had three children of their own, two daughters close in age to Oh'Dar, but Is'Taqa's son was still very young, and it would be years before he could learn the Brothers' ways. Oh'Dar was a fast learner, and Is'Taqa was more than happy to have the young man's company.

The Second Chief had taught him how to fish as the Brothers did. And because, unlike the People, Oh'Dar had no fear or resistance to water, he had become an accomplished swimmer. He would retrieve small shells and rocks from the rivers and the pond for Honovi's girls to add to their collection of pretty things. He was kind-hearted and took joy in seeing their delight with each new treasure he brought them. He helped sort them and pick out the best ones, and they loved having his undivided attention.

The Brothers had taught Oh'Dar to ride, and since this was a skill of which his mother would not approve, he had just never gotten around to telling her. Adia felt that horses were skittish and unpredictable, but they seemed to take easily to Oh'Dar. He excelled at nearly everything he attempted, and he loved learning. He was almost as good as their most accomplished rider, the young brave, Pajackok.

Is'Taqa had also taught Oh'Dar how to make bows and arrows—how to select the proper wood, how to bend it, and how to string it to the proper tension. He taught the young man which feathers worked best for the arrows. They spent countless afternoons together in target practice, and Oh'Dar had become an excellent marksman. Except, Oh'Dar was not one of the Brothers. And he was not one of the People either. And that was the problem gnawing him at his core that night.

Oh'Dar remembered the day he had first realized he was not like the People. He was sitting next to Acaraho on the banks of one of his favorite swimming places. Their reflection in the still waters caught his eye, and for the first time, he saw the glaring differences. The realization shattered his feeling of belonging. Odd how it had not occurred to him before, because it was so obvious once he saw it.

Why did I not notice how pale and smooth my skin is

compared to the skin of all the People, which is covered with soft down? How did I not notice how skinny my arms and legs are compared to theirs? Not see that my fingernails are practically useless?

And he could not see so well in the dark; he could not hear the forest sounds as well as they did. Neither could he identify animals by their scent at the distances the People could. In every way, his physical attributes paled against theirs, and from the time he realized his differences, he had never felt the same.

When he was with the Brothers, he did not feel so conspicuous. The young people of his age were of similar height and build. Even his dark hair was the same. And in the summer, his skin would darken almost to match the tones of theirs. Only his piercing blue eyes gave him away. He could blend in with the Brothers.

Is'Taqa had noticed that Oh'Dar was not himself lately. The young man had been sitting in silence for some time, chin in hand.

Something is bothering him more than the usual ups and downs. He has always been such a happy child, so full of joy. Yet, as he gets older, he is withdrawing more often; he shuts everyone else out.

Is'Taqa was concerned it was more than normal growing pains.

He continued to watch Oh'Dar and decided to ask Honovi if she had tasks the young man could help her with tomorrow. Perhaps she could draw him out and discover what was troubling him so. She and Oh'Dar had a special relationship going back to the days when she had spent long stretches at a time with the People, teaching him Whitespeak.

Is'Taqa's eldest daughter, Acise, sat across from Oh'Dar as he looked at nothing, lost in thought. She picked up an acorn cap and tossed it in his direction. It landed just in front of his feet. He noticed, looked up, and gave her a fake angry frown, at which she laughed and threw another.

The three of them sat around the crackling fire for quite a while longer. The murky night covered them like a blanket, concealing the usually bright stars. In the distance, owls hooted from the nearby Sycamore trees. Coyotes yipped and howled across the hills. Is'Taqa was filled with gratitude at how rich his life had become, and he counted his many blessings.

He stirred the fire one last time. Honovi came up to join them, "Snana and Noshoba are in bed. It is time for you to come in too now, Acise. You have already stayed up longer than your privileges as the eldest allow."

"Mama, but this is the best part," Acise replied.

Spending time with the adults around the evening fire was one of Acise's favorite things to do. She was fascinated with Oh'Dar, and she loved it when he visited. She had a special place, separate from her other treasures, where she kept the collections of shells he brought. When her parents permitted, she would follow Oh'Dar and her father around, just to be near the young man. Aside from her general fascination, she found in him the big brother she did not have.

"Now," was all Honovi had to say. Acise, knowing better than to argue, promptly arose, said goodnight to her father and Oh'Dar, and headed to the family shelter. Honovi was a loving and patient mother, except when it came to rebellious children. They knew better than to push her too far with their protestations.

Soon, Acise was bedded down with the others, safe and snug as Honovi waited for her mate and Oh'Dar to join them.

Always cold in the caves of Kthama, Oh'Dar soaked up the warmth of the fire radiating over his bare skin. In this, the slowly warming weather, Oh'Dar wore lighter cotton coverings, as did the Brothers, usually leaving most of his chest and arms bare. He was excited that Is'Taqa had promised to teach him some time before the cold weather to prepare hides and furs so he could make his own warm wrappings. The Brothers had been generous in providing coverings for Oh'Dar ever since he was tiny. But now that he was nearly grown, he had his own ideas of what he wanted to wear; he was anxious next to apply his creativity to sewing.

The People did not need heavy wrappings. The females wore a top covering to protect their modesty, and some with lighter undercoats chose to wear lower garments as well. Others wore them just for fashion and for a change.

The older man and the younger sat in silence a while longer. There was something sacred about sitting silently under the dark sky together, and Is'Taqa did not want to break the spell. Finally, the fire was reduced to burning embers. He looked over at Oh'Dar, who at last smiled at him in return. Is'Taqa smothered the last of the flames, and they retired to join the others.

Oh'Dar woke in the middle of the night to find that Acise had moved her sleeping mat to snuggle up against him. He tucked her blankets around her and lay back down, letting her rest up against his back.

The next morning, before Oh'Dar and the children were up, Is'Taqa spoke with Honovi about the young man's moods. "Have you noticed that he slips into his silences more and more lately?"

"Yes. And I am sure Adia has noticed it and is also worried," she answered.

"I wonder if you have some things today that he can help you with? Perhaps he will open up to you?"

"I will be glad to try and see how it goes. I will ask Acise to watch Snana and Noshoba," she replied.

Honovi had spring planting to do and would be glad for Oh'Dar's help and company.

The two set out shortly thereafter. "Here, let me carry your basket of seeds and plantings," offered Oh'Dar.

"Thank you. It's going to take us most of the day to finish this. I am glad we are getting an early start while it is still cool. Luckily, we have already prepared the ground. Part of it is in the sun and part in the shade, so we can plant these accordingly."

"I enjoy doing this. Thank you for inviting me."

"You have learned so much, Oh'Dar. You already know the plants your mother and Nadiwani use and how to create their preparations and tinctures. You have been learning our ways for almost as long, and I suspect that with the combination, you know more than any one of us," she joked.

"It is a shame that Healers cannot be male. But maybe I could be a Helper, at least? I do not know."

The two walked on in silence the rest of the way. The Brothers' territory met the People's along the far lower border, then stretched for vast distances in the other directions. The People had placed watchers high in the trees and at different elevations since the threat of the White Men, as they called themselves, had surfaced years ago. However, the Brothers had no such outposts. They were not particularly in need of them because the Waschini knew of their existence.

But the Waschini did not know of the existence

of the Sasquatch—either the legendary hulking giants or the offshoot hybrid population called the People.

Oh'Dar had never seen any Sasquatch other than the People. In fact, he had no idea that any other Sasquatch existed. Not being one of the select circle who carried the dark secrets of the past, he did not know the stories about how, out of desperation to avoid extinction, the Sarnonn Nu'numics had mated with the Brothers, producing the modified race of the People. The People were smaller than the Sarnonn but bigger and stronger than the Brothers, and they did not have the heavy coats of hair that the Sarnonn had. There were other physical differences, and for the most part, the People evidenced the best of both bloodlines. Though there had never been any voluntary matings between the Brothers and the People, each could regard the other as attractive.

However, the People were still different enough that the Waschini would not mistake them for the Brothers. And the Waschini had proven they sought to destroy that which they did not understand.

Back in his quarters, Khon'Tor was still lost in thought about his need to produce an offspring as heir to his leadership, when he was disturbed by a clack on the stone door of his living quarters. When he pulled the huge door open, there stood Akule.

Khon'Tor let out a big sigh when he saw the watcher; Akule always seemed to bring him bad news. But Akule knew critical information about the night Khon'Tor had attacked Adia, and the Leader had either to stay in Akule's good graces or kill him. Since Khon'Tor had not been able to make up his mind all these years, Akule was once more standing before him, interrupting his personal time.

"Adik'Tar, one of the outpost watchers has reported two Waschini riding through on horseback, near the Brothers' territory," he reported.

Khon'Tor told Akule that they would go together to notify Acaraho. The High Protector had guards and some watchers working in the field in preparation for the female's spring planting. He knew there were none near where the outpost had spotted the Waschini, but he was not sure if there were others assigned duties in the outer regions.

They found Acaraho still sitting with Adia in the Great Chamber. Both were getting up to leave when Khon'Tor and the watcher approached.

The balance of power had shifted since Hakani's death. Acaraho knew that Khon'Tor had attacked and violated Adia, and as a result, had fathered Nootau. Had Adia not stopped Acaraho on the day Hakani intentionally walked off the cliff, Acaraho would have killed Khon'Tor then and there. So, though they had come to a truce of sorts, there was still a great deal of tension between the two giants.

Never one for self-repudiation, Khon'Tor still

blamed Adia for his problems. Somehow in his twisted thinking, it was still her fault that he had attacked her. He felt no gratitude to her for not turning him in; he only resented the complication that she created in his life.

So, ignoring Adia, Khon'Tor looked at Acaraho. "One of the watchers spotted two Waschini riding through the edge of our territory. They should be passing through the Brothers' land shortly."

Acaraho thought for a moment. "I do not see a threat to us if they did not see our watcher. Akule?" Acaraho looked at im for confirmation.

Akule replied, "Kajika said there was no way anyone saw him. He observed them at a reasonable distance and was concealed in the trees."

Khon'Tor relaxed. If Acaraho was not concerned, then Khon'Tor was not either. Despite the tension between them, he still respected the High Protector's judgment and capabilities.

"Very well then, thank you, Commander," and with that, Khon'Tor turned and left, never acknowledging Adia's presence.

Acaraho and Adia looked at each other the moment Khon'Tor's back was to them.

"Oh'Dar," they signed to each other simultaneously.

CHAPTER 2

Honovi and Oh'Dar busied themselves with planting row after row of Corn Flower, Chamomile, Eucalyptus, and Fennel. As they worked, Honovi waited for an opening to broach the subject of Oh'Dar's pensive moods.

"I truly appreciate your help today," she started. "We always look forward to your visits; you are a blessing to us all."

Oh'Dar glanced over at her and smiled, crinkling up his eyes. Honovi was relieved to see the smile, not always being able to understand this sometimes-sullen young man before her. Where was the smiling, giggling, arm-flapping little boy she had helped raise?

"I do not mean to intrude, but you seem bothered by something. Would you like to talk about it? Is it anything I can help you with? Both Is'Taqa and I have noticed you are not yourself lately, and we want to make sure you are alright," she continued.

"I am fine. Sometimes I do not know where I fit in; that is all," he answered.

Honovi looked at Oh'Dar with concern in her eyes.

Such a heavy burden for such young shoulders to bear, she thought to herself.

She knew that both Adia and Nadiwani struggled over this exact possibility. They knew that, however much they taught him about living as one of the People, he would always be different.

They hoped his spending time with the Brothers would give him another family with whom he might identify a little closer since their physical differences were not so great. Had it not been for his startling blue eyes, with the summer darkening of his skin he could pass as one of them.

Honovi secretly expected that in a few years, when he came of pairing age, he would select a mate from the Brothers. There really was no other choice. She could see that he would be attractive, and with all the skills the People and the Brothers were teaching him, he would be a desirable mate—despite being Waschini.

Suddenly, as Honovi and Oh'Dar were speaking, the sound of hooves pounding the ground broke the air. They knew it could be that some of the Brothers were coming their way, but the cadence signaled people in a great hurry, and that meant either something grievous had happened or—*Waschini*.

Not taking chances, both Honovi and Oh'Dar headed for the protective cover of the nearby brush. It would be risky for a female to be caught isolated, and the Waschini must never learn about Oh'Dar. Ducking undercover just in time, they watched silently as two men on horseback raced by on the hillside beyond. The Waschini always seemed to be in a hurry, but in this case, the rapid sound of their approach was what saved the two from discovery. Had the riders been casually sauntering by, they would no doubt inadvertently have taken Honovi and Oh'Dar by surprise.

"They're gone. I will go and get the basket we left back in the field," offered Oh'Dar.

"We are lucky they did not notice it. We should hurry. There might be others following; let's get back to the village," urged Honovi.

Is'Taqa was talking with Chief Ogima when he noticed their early return. He saw their concern and hurried body language and came over to help, taking Honovi's basket from her.

"What happened? You both look upset," he asked.

"Please, let's just go to our shelter," replied Honovi, shaken.

Realizing they wanted to have a private conversation, Oh'Dar went to find Acise and Snana.

Feeling safer secluded in their living area, Honovi told Is'Taqa what had happened.

He tried not to let on how concerned he was about the close encounter. Had they come across his mate and the young man, he was frightened by what the outcome might have been.

"We have heard the stories of the Waschini. I do not believe they are all evil—we know for a fact that Oh'Dar has a naturally good heart and gentle disposition—but other than him, there are only stories of their dark deeds. No good ones." Is'Taqa was not going to take any chances—not with his own family, or anyone else's for that matter.

Honovi looked across at him. "I can see by the look on your face that you are more worried than you are letting on. I think Oh'Dar should return home until this has passed." Hoping Oh'Dar had not caught the furtive glances exchanged between them, she thought it best that the young man should return to the protection and sanctuary of Kthama.

"You are right, I am. I did not ever tell you, but not long after Adia rescued Oh'Dar, some Waschini entered the village and asked if there was a White infant here; if we had found one and were taking care of it. Not wanting a problem, Chief Ogima let them look through the village. Of course, the Chief could not expose the People, and Oh'Dar was at Kthama by then. Only Chief Ogima, my sister, and I knew about Oh'Dar at that point. There was no time to contact Adia and fetch him in secret, and if we had, the Waschini might well have accused us of kidnapping. There was also no way to ask where they had come from; at that point, we knew of no White settlements and were only able to discover they had traveled very far. It was a long time ago, but I remember it as if it were yesterday."

That evening, around the nightly fire, Is'Taqa stole a look at Honovi and raised his eyebrows in a question. Honovi nodded oh-so-slightly in agreement. They had been bonded long enough that they often understood each other without the need for words or Handspeak.

Is'Taqa spoke. "Oh'Dar, we need to return you to the People tomorrow. I want to talk to Acaraho about a few things anyway. We will head out at first light."

Oh'Dar frowned in disappointment. He was not ready to return. Though he could have objected if he'd had a valid reason, he knew better than to argue with his elders—whether one of the Brothers or one of the People. They did not tolerate disrespect from offspring, not even if they were already young adults. So he let it go, deciding to suggest another visit soon. He had already spent several weeks with them and was grateful for each one.

"Yes, Adik'Tar Is'Taqa," he answered, using the honorific for respect. "I will be ready."

The next morning, Is'Taqa and Oh'Dar set out very early to make their way back to Kthama. Learning from what direction the two Waschini riders had come, Is'Taqa made sure to take a circuitous route in case others were following. He wanted to make sure he delivered Oh'Dar safely into the People's hands.

Traveling with Oh'Dar is far easier than with Acaraho, Is'Taqa thought. *Even when Acaraho shortens his strides and pace, it is still hard work to keep up with him. Of course, the benefit is that he clears the path easily enough, whereas we have to work hard to do it.*

The People and the Brothers did not travel often enough between each others' settlements to create an established path, even when they took the familiar route. And now, with the Waschini threat, it would be very unwise to have a visible trail leading from the Brothers' village to anywhere near Kthama.

They made it by midday, and after exchanging greetings, Is'Taqa asked for Adia or Acaraho. Awan, the First Guard, was on duty at the time and went to find Adia, returning shortly with her in tow. When she saw them waiting for her, she hurried with relief across the stone floor of the Great Chamber.

The last thing any of them needed was for the Waschini to come across one of their own among the Brothers.

"Hello, Is'Taqa. Thank you for bringing Oh'Dar safely home," she said, placing an arm around her son's shoulders. "I am afraid that Acaraho left earlier to fetch him. He is probably already on his way back by now. Your people would have told him when he arrived that you had already left."

Oh'Dar thought it odd that his father would come to get him when both Adia and Acaraho had known he would be staying longer. He had thought the same when Is'Taqa decided the night before that they would travel to Kthama in the morning. Both the People and the Brothers had tried to keep the horror stories about the Waschini from Oh'Dar since he was technically one of them. But now the young man realized that there might have been more to Honovi's reaction than her fear of the riders themselves.

Acaraho had indeed already arrived at the Brothers' village and found out from Honovi that Is'Taqa had left earlier with Oh'Dar. He asked her what she had seen of the two riders, and she did not have much to report other than whereabouts on the upper trail she had seen them, and in what direction they were going. Still, he asked her to tell him every detail she could, regardless of how inconsequential she thought it might be.

Acaraho then thanked her and set out to find the trail she said the Waschini had traveled.

He had no trouble finding the path. He could still

see the hoof prints faintly in the soil. Waschini were the only ones whose horses left behind such a distinctive curved pattern. Realizing that Is'Taqa and Oh'Dar must be safely back at Kthama by now, Acaraho kept his eyes on the indentations and followed them along.

The more these incidents occurred, the more Acaraho wished the Brothers had watchers posted as he did. He knew it was not feasible. The Brothers' population was nothing compared to that of the People's, and they did not have men to spare for such positions. He made a mental note to ask for Chief Ogima's permission to place some of his watchers on their territory for their mutual benefit.

The Waschini had ridden with purpose; they clearly had a destination in mind, and Acaraho wanted very much to know what it was. He tracked the horses for some time, giving up only when the prints ended at a large open field. Remaining hidden among the trees was one thing, but crossing that expansive an area in broad daylight was not wise.

He abandoned the trail and followed his way back. Every fifty paces or so, he selected a four-year-old sapling and broke it at about waist height to mark the path for later. The unnatural twist and position of the break would be obvious to any of the People, but not to the Waschini.

The High Protector made it back to Kthama before twilight. Adia, Nadiwani, Oh'Dar, and Nootau were sitting together in the community eating area when he arrived.

Spring was an exhausting time, and most of the People took advantage of the community meals. The task of feeding a large group was still preferable to fixing individual meals in their living areas. The room was abuzz with talk about the work of the day and gratitude for the rich, dark soil, the sweet, humid scent of the spring blossoms hanging in the air, the lilting birdsong serenading from the trees. Etera was reawakening in the Great Mother's promise of continual renewal.

Acaraho sat down, straddling the rock bench to sit next to Nootau. Clearly distracted by his thoughts, Acaraho's brows knitted together tensely. He was sorry he had missed Is'Taqa; he would have liked to broach the possibility of placing watchers along the route the Waschini had traveled.

Looking across at Oh'Dar sandwiched between the two females, he was struck anew with just how frail the young man was in comparison. He had his concerns about Oh'Dar's future among the People, but usually, he put them out of his mind and committed again to doing the best he could in raising the boy. Considering the stories of the Waschini, perhaps Oh'Dar was safer there among all these powerful peaceful giants than he would be among the heartless White Wasters, even though they were of his own kind.

Nadiwani caught the several hurried glances between Adia and Acaraho. When they had finished eating, she rose up and said, "Come on, Oh'Dar and Nootau, let's go straighten up the mess I left earlier. I could use your help."

Adia and Acaraho both smiled and nodded a word of thanks to her for providing them some time alone. Nadiwani put one hand on a shoulder of each offspring and escorted them away with her.

Acaraho rubbed his hand over his mouth as he often did when thinking. He could feel Adia impatiently staring a hole in him as she waited for him to talk to her.

"I found the path the riders traveled. I followed it for some distance but abandoned the trail when it crossed an open field. I may send some watchers after dark," he said.

"What did you find out that is bothering you, Acaraho, despite the obvious?"

"I asked Honovi to tell me everything she could about the riders, even though she only caught a glimpse. From what she said, their horses were only partially laden. It tells me that if wherever they were going was a fair distance by horseback, there are places close enough for them to replenish their supplies as they travel, or where they were going is close and was their end goal. Either way, it means that there are others in the area only some distance past where Honovi saw them," he explained finally.

Adia sighed, glad that Acaraho had finally said what was bothering him. She now understood his disquiet. Whether there was a temporary encampment or a permanent establishment, it meant that others would possibly be following their route. The riders had ridden with intent toward their destination, one they knew would be there waiting for them. The word was that it was in this way that they branched across the land; by establishing stopping-off points and from there extending their ingress by another length.

The People were not naturally aggressive. Their intent was to live in peace with all the Great Spirit's creations. But the Waschini were aggressive, and Acaraho would have to let both Khon'Tor and the other High Council members know of this encroachment.

Adia ran her eyes over Acaraho as he returned to his thoughts. How she longed to go and put her arms around him. He had so much responsibility on his shoulders, and on top of that, he had taken on raising her two offspring. They were as much a family—in all the ways that defined a family—as any of the others in the community. But through all the years, she still had not found a way to quench her longing to be with him as his mate. They had learned to control their desire for each other by starving it off, allowing only the briefest of physical contact between them—a passing squeeze of a hand, perhaps a brief resting of one on a shoulder. But what they denied each other during the daytime both tried to make up in their imaginations at night.

Acaraho turned and looked around the room. Most of the others had left by now. Khon'Tor was not in his usual eating area.

"In the morning, I will have to let Khon'Tor know of my concerns. In the meantime, let me walk you back to your Quarters, Healer."

The two walked in silence, savoring the last few moments of each other's company. Acaraho always accompanied Adia to her Quarters, each simultaneously reaching for and clasping the other's hand for the briefest moment as they reached her door.

Once Adia was safely inside, Acaraho returned to his quarters and drifted off to sleep with tender thoughts of Adia and longing for that which would never be theirs to share.

Years before, Nadiwani had warned Acaraho about the path the two were taking. She knew they cared for each other deeply, but a Healer could never mate, and Acaraho was a robust male who himself had never mated. She feared they were asking more of themselves than was realistically possible, but some-how, it seemed they had never crossed the line. Nadi-wani was also forbidden to mate, but she was not presented every day with the object of her desire within arm's reach.

Nadiwani was right—Acaraho and Adia had never crossed the line, but they were tortured by their longing for each other. Though forbidden to her, Adia knew that any of the females would jump at the chance to be Acaraho's mate. She caught how their eyes followed him around the room. If she allowed her thoughts to linger on him for very long—how he towered over most of the People, his expansive shoulders, his broad chest, his dark warm eyes, his strong jawline, his muscular thighs—she would suffer another fitful, sleepless night. She struggled with the thought of abandoning her role as Healer. She was also plagued with guilt that he was giving up for her one of the pleasures of being a male.

Adia had never established a Connection with Acaraho despite the ability taught to her by Urilla Wuti from the People of the Far High Hills. Urilla Wuti was the Healer who had come to help Adia deliver her twins, Nootau and Nimida. Then Urilla Wuti had taken Nimida back with her to hide the offspring's existence in what was a highly inflamma-tory and dangerous situation at Kthama.

Only once had Adia used her Connection skills with Acaraho. She had sent him a message of intense love, breaking through his rage and stopping him from murdering Khon'Tor at the path's edge where Hakani had just taken her own life. Adia had not done it for Khon'Tor's sake. She had feared that Acaraho would be filled with remorse that it was he who had killed Nootau's natural father.

Before falling asleep, Adia asked Oh'Dar if he had enjoyed his visit with Is'Taqa and Honovi. He told her he had but was disappointed to return home so suddenly.

Impulsively, she hugged him and said, "You know, when you were little, Nadiwani and I used to marvel at your creativity. You would combine stacking toys in ways none of the other offspring thought of. And you were always coming up with new uses for everyday items. Even the other females would stare at you and marvel at your inventiveness.

"I see in use everywhere around Kthama the large water baskets that you came up with. Because your weaves were so fine, we no longer have to use the inconvenient, small baskets for our daily water. Everyone remarks that your woven patterns are better than anyone else's. And now, because of you, nearly every living area has more than enough water for each family's daily needs. That one innovation alone has saved everyone a great deal of work carting water back and forth from the Mother Stream. You should be proud of yourself, Oh'Dar. I know I am."

Lying on his sleeping mat, Oh'Dar was glad to be home, and at the same time, he was not. He had missed Adia, who was his mother in all respects, and he was glad she was proud of him. He was also pleased to see Nootau. But the minute he was back among the People, he was again starkly reminded that he was an Outsider. And no matter how much he loved them and they loved him in return, there was unrest inside him that their love could not soothe.

Oh'Dar turned over on his side and spied the stuffed bear that Adia had told him she found when she rescued him. Tattered and worn, it was still his favorite toy. He was far too old for toys, but he did not care. He loved his bear, and it was a comfort to him. He hugged it close, shut his eyes, and tried to sleep.

The next morning, Acaraho told Khon'Tor how he had followed the Waschini tracks and his belief that there would be others traveling the same route eventually. Acaraho also told Khon'Tor of his intention to approach Ogima Adoeete, the High Chief of the

Brothers, and Second Chief Is'Taqa, about posting watchers along the suspected Waschini travel route crossing the Brothers' territory.

As Khon'Tor replied, Acaraho was indulging in a vision of his hands around Khon'Tor's throat. Acaraho was never near the Leader without having to resist the desire to snap his neck, but he had a duty to honor his position as High Protector. For the sake of the People, he had promised Adia he would not harm Khon'Tor. And he had learned to control that desire, just as he had learned to suppress his longing for Adia. Acaraho was often exhausted at night from fighting urges that severely tested his self-control.

He recognized that Khon'Tor had so far shown great restraint in not invoking Wrak-Ayya, the Age of Shadows, at the High Rocks. Wrak-Ayya was foretold by the Ancients and would usher in harsh changes necessary to ensure the continuation of the People. The High Council had mapped out several stages of Wrak-Ayya. The lowest levels created minimal impact on day-to-day living, but as the threat rose, the effect on the People's lives and routines would also rise. Each Leader had to decide for himself when and if to invoke stages of Wrak-Ayya. It was a weighty decision.

"—my hope is that it will be generations before the Age of Shadows falls," said Khon'Tor, "But if what you believe is true, I may well be forced to invoke Wrak-Ayya in my lifetime."

Acaraho and several of his watchers traced the Waschini tracks partway back to where they had come from. The riders had only crossed one border of the People's territory before crossing into that of the Brothers.

Before too much time had passed, Acaraho met with Ogima Adoeete and Is'Taqa. They agreed to let Acaraho post some of the watchers along the route that the riders had traveled. Chief Ogima was glad for Acaraho's help. Though there had not yet been problems between the Waschini and the Brothers, having the watchers in place benefited both tribes.

Is'Taqa was particularly grateful for Acaraho's suggestion. It made him nervous that Honovi and Oh'Dar had been out alone that day. Should a similar situation arise, Is'Taqa knew that none of the People would allow any harm to come to anyone— People or Brothers—under their watch.

Not long after, Acaraho sent several of his watchers to follow the tracks across the open field from where he had left off following the riders. They easily picked up the Waschini trail on the other side and followed it for days under cover of darkness. During the day, they remained concealed—a defensive tactic they were exceptionally good at—and started again at nightfall. They repeated the same tree breaks to indicate the path as Acaraho had.

Finally, after many days' travel, from the top of a high crest, they spotted lights far down in the valley below. It was not campfire light; it was coming from inside many varied structures. Horses whinnied and neighed, perhaps picking up the watchers' scent from above them. The males turned back and reported to Acaraho what they had found. Though the place was many days from the Brothers' territory and many days farther from the People's, Acaraho still found its existence unsettling.

Summer progressed uneventfully. Oh'Dar spent more and more time with Is'Taqa and Honovi. As Oh'Dar had asked, Is'Taqa taught him how to tan deer hide into leather. Honovi showed him how to fashion small bones into sewing needles and what to use for thread. She also taught him how to make moccasins and weave soft undergarments from cotton. Now that he could make his own clothes, he would no longer be dependent on the Brothers' hand-me-downs.

With each new skill, Oh'Dar moved a step forward in his independence. Though he was a male, he had no compunction about learning to sew. Next season he hoped to learn how to spin the thread from cotton. He had an unquenchable thirst for knowledge and soaked up whatever they or his people were willing to teach him.

Acaraho went to meet Oh'Dar when it was time for the young man to return to Kthama. Oh'Dar had a large stack of hides and skins to bring back to work on through the winter months when most of the People moved their attention to indoor activities. Acaracho traversed the steep incline to the meeting spot where Is'Taqa was waiting.

"Hello, Acaraho!" Is'Taqa raised his hand as he shouted out the greeting.

"Is'Taqa! It is good to see you again. How are Honovi and your offspring?" he asked, his strong legs easily carrying him down the slope to Is'Taqa's side.

"Everyone is well. It has been a bountiful harvest this year, and we are looking forward to a break over the upcoming cooler months," replied the Chief.

Acaraho followed him to the Brothers' village where Oh'Dar was waiting. Oh'Dar was sitting with Honovi, Acise, Snana, and the young Noshoba, who was asleep on a soft pelt at their feet. He was helping Acise string some shells into a necklace for her mother.

It was unusual for one of the People to enter the village in broad daylight, but Acaraho had come to carry Oh'Dar's supplies. Easily eight feet tall, Acaraho towered over Is'Taqa—who himself was tall for one of the Brothers. As they approached, nearly everyone stopped what they were doing and turned to look. Acise and Snana watched, transfixed. Their eyes widened as Acaraho drew near. Little Noshoba, just a toddler, slept through his arrival, unimpressed. Acaraho, the male who had raised Oh'Dar as his own son, was now entering the camp in broad daylight.

To Oh'Dar, Acaraho was his father coming to pick him up, not the legendary Acaraho, High Protector of the People of the High Rocks. He looked around at the Brothers' reactions and was dumbstruck. For the first time, he saw his father through their eyes.

Honovi stood up and greeted Acaraho. Wanting to reassure her children that he was a friend, she took his hand and led him closer to the two girls.

Most of the contact between the two tribes involved only the Leaders, and that usually under cover of darkness. Even though Ithua and Adia were good friends and exchanged knowledge and supplies, Adia rarely appeared openly in or around the Brothers' village.

Acaraho ignored the open stares of the Brothers. He realized that he was a novelty to them and was glad for the opportunity to demonstrate his good intent.

Seeing that the girls were not afraid, he crouched

down next to them, making it a point to do so very slowly.

Snana, the younger, put out her hand and ran it down his shoulder and over his arm, petting the soft undercoat. She smiled from ear to ear and said, "Bunny, soft, big, man!" to which everyone laughed out loud.

With that, the tension was broken, and everyone relaxed a bit.

Acaraho saw the gigantic pile of wraps over to one side. Oh'Dar indeed had a considerable stock of hides and furs. It was no matter for Acaraho to carry them back, but he could see why they had not moved them closer to the meeting place and why he had needed to enter the village.

Pointing at the stack and smiling, Acaraho asked, "Is that all?" Everyone laughed at his joke.

"I cannot wait for Mama to see it!" exclaimed Oh'Dar. Acaraho was happy to see him so proud of his accomplishments.

"Oh'Dar is always an exemplary student, Acaraho," replied Is'Taqa. "We have been talking about what he might like to learn this summer," he added.

"Your mother will be anxious to hear everything you plan to learn, Oh'Dar," said Acaraho. He knew that Adia's heartfelt desire was for Oh'Dar to grow in his abilities and find his place in the world.

As they were still talking, three wolf cubs ambled over in their direction. Acise and Snana laughed as the cubs jumped all over them, happily covering their faces with puppy kisses.

"What is up with these little things?" asked Acaraho. It was not unusual for the Brothers to take in wolf cubs and keep them as pets, though it was odd to see any this young.

"Unfortunately, one of the wolves we trapped had young. We rescued them and brought them here," Is'Taqa explained.

One of the cubs was now clamoring around Oh'Dar, jumping onto his legs, hoping to be picked up. Oh'Dar reached down and retrieved the little bundle of fur, hugging the fluffy creature to his neck and stroking it gently.

"*Uh-oh*," thought Acaraho. It was obvious that this one had become Oh'Dar's cub! He heaved a huge sigh. It was not unheard of for the People to keep pets, but usually, they were rabbits and small reptiles and only kept for short periods. Acaraho was uncertain what Adia would say, but he knew he did not have the heart to deny the boy if Oh'Dar asked to bring the cub back with him. Acaraho decided that if he had to, he would keep it in his bachelor quarters.

Oh'Dar looked over at his father, his eyes begging to be able to keep the cub.

Acaraho could not help but chuckle. "Alright," he smiled, "But do not dare leave me alone when it's time to tell your mother!" he joked.

Oh'Dar broke out in a huge smile, the little cub still covering his face with kisses.

"Are you ready to head back?" Acaraho asked.

Oh'Dar gave Honovi and each of the girls a hug, though Acise held onto him for longer than her mother and sister did. Is'Taqa came over and put his arm around Oh'Dar's shoulder.

Acaraho easily scooped up the huge pile and turned to head back to Kthama. He let Oh'Dar take the lead and set the pace, the cub secured in a sling specifically fashioned for carrying him. Acaraho smiled to himself; the young man had anticipated his permission to bring the wolf back with them.

As they walked together, a swell of gratitude rose in Oh'Dar's chest. He was pleased about everything he was learning from the Brothers, but Acaraho had taught him even more.

"Father, I've been thinking about all the time you spent with Nootau and me when we were growing up. I remember lying outside at night, looking up at the bright sky while you explained the phases of the moon and how to navigate using it and the stars, and how the night sky shows us what to plant when. And you taught us how to tell the different calls of the night birds. I still cannot pick up Etera's magnetic fields, like you taught Nootau. That sure must be handy for navigation, but I do not think I will ever be able to do that."

Acaraho had helped each find his own gifts and had taught Oh'Dar and Nootau to be proud of their differences instead of comparing themselves with each other. And he taught them that, as brothers, they should help and lean on each other as their differing skills allowed.

He told them the stories from the Ancients that had been passed down for generations from father to son. He played hunting games with them that taught them how to think strategically. He taught them how to fashion tools, how to defend themselves, and, if necessary, how to fight.

Acaraho had always made sure there was no direct competition between the two boys. He knew that in any show of strength, Oh'Dar would not stand a chance against Nootau, but that when it came to innovation and creativity, Nootau would not stand a chance against Oh'Dar.

"Though I am learning a lot from Is'Taqa and the Brothers, I am grateful for all the time you spend with us." Oh'Dar stopped and turned back to face Acaraho, adding, "No one could ask for a better father."

"And no one could ask for a better son," smiled Acaraho in return. "But *you're* still telling your mother about the wolf cub," he added before they continued.

They made it back to Kthama in reasonable time. They'd had to stop and let the little cub out now and then, which slowed them down a bit.

Once back at Kthama, Acaraho carried the pile of

hides and furs into the Great Chamber and plopped them down on one of the largest tables for the meantime.

Some of the females came over, not only to welcome them back but out of curiosity over the high pile of wrappings Acaraho had just offloaded. Because many of the females wore wrappings, they were curious about the volume and rich array of materials—and what Oh'Dar might do with them considering his unusual skills.

Mapiya, who had sat with Oh'Dar many times while he was growing up, was one of the females to come over. She hugged him and remarked on how handsome he looked.

Oh'Dar flipped through the skins, peeling up a corner of each so they could see them more easily. The females oohed and aahed over each one, especially the thick, soft wolf pelts.

As she examined them, Mapiya felt something licking her arm and jumped. Oh'Dar's wolf cub had managed to get his head out of the carrying sling and was affectionately greeting her. Now all the females had to pass the cub around and cuddle it.

Acaraho was very happy to see his son enjoying the attention and looking so relaxed.

Finally, Adia, Nadiwani, and Nootau showed up and came rushing over to greet the returning family members.

Adia's heart was heavy that Oh'Dar had been away so much, but she wanted the boy to be happy; however that had to be. She knew he was a big help to Honovi and Ithua, and that he was learning a great deal during his stays there.

Though it was surely not possible in only a few weeks, Adia was certain that Oh'Dar had grown. He was taking on more and more of the Brothers' characteristics and letting his straight black hair grow long. Only his blue eyes gave him away.

She smiled and nodded her approval at the pile of hides, knowing how important it was for Oh'Dar to learn how to make his own clothes.

Kthama is too cold for him during the cooler months. He is so creative; I wonder what he'll come up with using these heavier skins?

Based on the improvements Oh'Dar had made to other things around Kthama, Adia did not doubt that his sewing would be of interest to others.

The females who wear wrappings will be anxious to talk to him about his new skill. I am sure many would appreciate some more delicate designs!

Suddenly, someone pressed a fluffy bundle of squirming wolf cub into her hands. She startled, then laughed and grabbed it up to her face, letting it cover her with licky kisses. Seeing her son's beaming face, she could not be angry, though she did pretend to squint angrily at Acaraho.

She had lived through Oh'Dar's younger days, which he spent getting into everything in their Quarters and turning it all upside down, and she guessed she could get through this, seeing how happy the cub made her son.

Oh, how I hope it is broken to outside, she thought to herself, reasonably positive it was not.

Nootau waited impatiently for his turn to hold the cub. "What did you name him?" he asked his brother.

"Kweeuu," replied Oh'Dar. They laughed at his unusual lack of creativity in naming the cub *Wolf*.

"It looks as if you are going to have a busy season," said Acaraho to Oh'Dar. "I think it is time we convert one of the extra rooms into a workshop for you. That way, you can spread all your tools and supplies out and not have to pack them up all the time," he explained.

"Really, Father? Oh, that would be great. Thank you!" replied Oh'Dar.

Adia looked hopefully at her son's beaming face and thought perhaps things would turn around for him now.

Having nothing else on his agenda for the day, Acaraho said, "Let's go down there now and pick one out, and then this afternoon I can help you set things up. I imagine you will need work tables and seating. Maybe we should install beams overhead for you to hang materials from."

Nootau spoke up, "I want to help!" And so the three of them went off to select a workroom for Oh'Dar.

Adia felt the sting of tears welling in her eyes, her heart full of hope that this might be the start of her odd-man-out Waschini son finding his place in the community.

Acaraho, Oh'Dar, and Nootau—with some help from a couple of other males—spent the rest of the afternoon starting to set up Oh'Dar's workshop. Under Acaraho's guidance, they had selected a room not far from the Healer's Quarters, and like hers, along an outer wall so they could make light tunnels to brighten the room. Because Oh'Dar lacked the People's better low light vision, Acaraho wanted to make sure that he would have use of the room for as much of the day as possible. Mapiya and Haiwee offered to whitewash it with chalk to lighten it further after the males finished setting up the tables, seating, and shelves. Phosphorescent rocks would provide some light after dark.

Oh'Dar beamed with excitement. He had never thought of having a room of his own. There he could lay out all his materials without having to pack and unpack constantly, trying to keep them out of everyone else's way. The helpers let him tell them where he wanted everything placed, allowing him to make it truly his own.

The room was going to come together much more easily than expected. "As long as the weather holds up over the next few days, we will work on digging the light tunnels," explained Acaraho, his arm around Oh'Dar's shoulders as they stood admiring their accomplishment.

"As soon as all the digging is done, we'll lighten the walls for you, Oh'Dar," Mapiya reminded him.

The females could not be working while the males were. Poking up through the ceiling to create the first channel was likely to bring all sorts of debris into the room—not to mention the mess when they dug the shaft.

Adia was dying to see what they had done, but she also knew that Oh'Dar would want to show her himself when it was finally ready. She paced around the room, leaving her work undone.

Meanwhile, Kweeuu was making short work of the leaves and stems that had dropped from the worktable. She watched as Nadiwani peeked underneath to see him shredding them into a million pieces, his little tail going a mile a minute.

Adia smiled. She was happy to have him occupied, hoping he would tire himself out before it was time to turn in. Between Oh'Dar's new projects and caring for this cub, she was hoping he would be busy enough to keep his mind off his troubles.

Finally, after just a few days, the workroom was complete.

Acaraho and the others who had helped, waited in the room to share in the celebration while Oh'Dar went to fetch Adia and Nadiwani.

He took each by the hand to lead them to the workroom. Kweeuu followed happily along, stopping to sniff the walls and pathway every few feet, then running quickly to catch up.

"Close your eyes, and no peeking until I tell you to look," said Oh'Dar. Then, "Now!" he announced, and the two opened their eyes and looked around.

They stared in amazement. It was an inviting workspace. The usual stone door had been replaced with a wooden one that Oh'Dar could easily open and close. There was a huge stone worktable situated under two light tunnels, just as one was arranged in the Healer's Quarters. Three massive beams traversed overhead, no doubt for hanging and drying items.

Across the back wall were more large tables. Acaraho had brought in the skins and hides, and Oh'Dar had divided them with like stacked upon like. Another beam spanned the back wall, again, probably for drying items, including sinew for thread. In one corner was a contraption made of wooden poles lashed together, used to stretch and dry the hides.

The chalk on the wall lightened everything. Adia could see that Oh'Dar had put a lot of thought into the layout. Being converted living quarters, it had all the comforts Oh'Dar would need to spend hours and hours there enjoying himself. And located where it was, he could easily find his way back to their Quarters, even through the darkened tunnels.

Adia clasped her hands and exclaimed, "Oh'Dar, It is truly wonderful. You did a great job."

"Thank you, Mama. I helped with some of the lighter work, but I mostly just said where to put things. Acaraho and Awan and the others did all the heavy work," he replied humbly.

Kweeuu had caught up by now and ran happily over to Oh'Dar. The cub did not pay the room any notice but was thrilled to see his young master. Oh'Dar picked him up and signed to him that he was a good cub.

Nadiwani remarked, "You're teaching him Handspeak?"

"Yes! I started at the Brothers' village. Watch!" And he plopped the cub gently back down on the floor in front of him.

Oh'Dar signed, "Sit," and Kweeuu sat. Oh'Dar signed, "Roll over," and the cub rolled over. Everyone laughed freely, never having thought to try teaching tricks to a pet—and using Handspeak, no less.

"He also knows *no*, *good cub*, and *outside*, Oh'Dar explained.

Nadiwani laughed, "Well, I wish I had known about *no* when he was shredding all the roots and leaves under the worktable!"

The lighthearted spirit within the group lifted Adia's heart.

Later, back in the Healer's Quarters, Nadiwani took out Oh'Dar's Keeping Stone and marked the day his workshop was finished. She stopped for a moment to reflect on the trials and joys of the years that had passed. It was hard to believe that Oh'Dar was almost a grown man. In a few years, if he were not already, he would be thinking of taking a mate.

CHAPTER 3

Within a few short months, the cooler air had set in. Oh'Dar busied himself with making warmer full-length coverings for himself. He had learned from Honovi how to dye the skins, turning them a beautiful soft brown. He fashioned warm moccasins for himself as well as various carrying belts. When he was done, he admired his work and felt prepared to winter over in Kthama's cool rooms and corridors.

As it did every year, the People spent more time inside socializing through the cold months.

This meant it was harder for Khon'Tor to avoid Adia and her son. He did not like the reminders and especially did not like the fact that Adia knew that she was his intended First Choice—thanks to

Hakani, who had blurted it out before she died. He wished she had taken that information to the grave with her. That Adia knew he had initially wanted her as his mate must give her some kind of hold over him.

Khon'Tor was sitting in his usual spot in the room when Adia and Nootau entered. He scowled unconsciously at the young male as he looked for signs of himself. He did not know the offspring because he tried to avoid him and his mother, but Khon'Tor indulged himself this time. He admitted that he could see parts of himself in Nootau, who had grown over the summer, and the Leader realized the young male would soon be of pairing age.

The boy will eventually have my height. Time will tell if he will inherit my build.

The thought that Nootau would be ready to mate within a few years gave Khon'Tor pause, however.

Has that much time passed? If I am going to produce an heir, I will have to do something soon. I am sure many are wondering why I have not taken another mate.

The People knew that he and Hakani were estranged off and on throughout their relationship. No-one could believe that he was still too grief-stricken to select another partner. Khon'Tor wondered; if he picked the youngest female allowable, could he bend her ignorance to his desires. He doubted he could even perform any more without the excitement that domination brought him.

How would she know any better? he thought.

Couples would flirt with each other, occasionally pressing the line of propriety, but they did not openly discuss mating practices. Those waiting to be paired were only taught about mating in preparatory sessions called the Ashwea Tare.

Adia noticed Khon'Tor watching them.

Does he ever regret not claiming Nootau? He still has not taken another mate, but he has to be thinking about it —though there is no guarantee his offspring would be male.

Adia did not let herself think about Nootau's sister, Nimida. She knew from Urilla Wuti that the girl was healthy and safe. She did not want to know more, lest the temptation to try to contact her daughter won out. Only a handful knew of her existence—Nadiwani, Acaraho, Urilla Wuti, and the two attendants who had helped smuggle the newborn offspring out of Kthama. Adia often struggled with the desire to claim Nimida and bring her home. But she still believed she had made the best, most unselfish decision to give Nimida a chance at a better life—a life free of any repercussions from Khon'Tor and without the risk of being burdened and shamed should the facts of her conception be revealed. Aside from that, if Adia had claimed Nimida, word would have reached the High Council members, and there was no doubt they would have forced her to give up the offspring and place her elsewhere anyway. Nimida was now almost grown up, and no good would come of ripping her from where Urilla Wuti had settled her.

Adia's thoughts turned to Oh'Dar. If Nootau would soon be of pairing age, so would Oh'Dar, though he seemed to be maturing more slowly than Nootau. She did not doubt Nootau's suitability to be paired. But Oh'Dar; that offspring's future had plagued them all from the beginning.

Where will he find a mate? The only possibility is one of the Brothers' maidens. Thanks to Acaraho and Is'Taqa, his skills are growing at a good rate, so he will have no trouble providing for a family should the opportunity for one arise.

Though she was living unpaired, it was not a path Adia would wish on her son—or anyone. True, it had been easier before she started noticing Acaraho, and they had begun to care for each other.

Adia struggled with the possibility of stepping down as Healer to become Acaraho's mate. Her skills were critical to the People, and she was renowned throughout all the People's communities for her gifts. To lose her as Healer would be devastating for many.

Do I have the right selfishly to choose a life as Acara- ho's mate over honoring my calling? And as far as I can tell, there are not yet any females among the offspring who have the Healer's gift and could become apprentices.

Adia did not know what to do, but she knew it was getting harder and harder to stop thinking about

Acaraho. At night, when all was quiet, she could not keep her thoughts from turning to him. She often struggled to fall asleep, her body filled with desire for his. She did not know how long this could continue. She was certain that Acaraho, too, was suffering. He never mentioned it, but she occasionally caught him watching her in an unguarded moment, the longing on his face telling her that he shared her struggles. She felt she owed it to them both somehow to find a way to end their misery. And sooner rather than later.

The day had finally come to an end. It had been productive, starting with meetings between Acaraho and the other males about the winter assignments. Repairs had to be done on the tunnels; the Gnoaii must be stocked. The females would need help bringing in the rest of the late harvest, and there were watcher and guard schedules to discuss.

There had been a few more sightings of Waschini riders passing through, though Acaraho imagined this would stop with the colder months approaching. He had seen how the Brothers and Oh'Dar struggled with the dropping temperatures every year. Traveling cross country fighting snow and ice would not be an easy journey for the Waschini. Acaraho expected that if their travels were going to pick up, it would be once the weather warmed.

Acaraho was very glad to get home to his quarters. He knew that at least tonight, he would be able to sleep, exhausted as he was. He did his best to keep his mind off Adia, though he usually indulged himself with thoughts of her when he was finally alone. But not tonight. Tonight, he needed a good night's sleep because tomorrow would not be any easier.

He drifted off to sleep immediately, only to be awakened a few hours later with the feeling that someone was in his room.

He opened his eyes to see a female figure standing near his sleeping mat. He could see the outline of her hair falling to her shoulders; he could see the curve of her waist above her hips. Her arms were resting at her sides, and she was standing there as if she had been watching him for some time.

Acaraho was not alarmed, but he could not fathom who she was, or how she could be in his quarters. Surely, he would have heard the stone door scrape against the floor as it opened? Surely he had not been *that* tired?

He raised himself on his elbows and was about to speak when she started to walk toward him. At that moment, he awakened enough to recognize Adia. *Adia! What is she doing here?*

Adia walked slowly over to where he was lying. She loosened her top wrap and let it fall to the floor behind her. Then she knelt over him, straddling his torso and placing her arms on either side of his chest. She lowered herself to him, and her breasts brushed against him, sending a shockwave through him that took his breath away. Before he could move, her lips were on his, and he could not help but respond. They exchanged their first kiss, at first sweet and soft, then yielding to their stored-up passion, deeper and longer. He could not believe she was there.

He knew he should be strong, but it was too late. He had wanted Adia for too long. As long as they did not cross the line, he could control himself—but this was beyond reason, beyond anyone's ability to resist. He encircled her with his arms and pulled her tightly against him. He ran his hands over her back and down to her hips, pressing them hard into his, his desire for her now past his control.

Then Acaraho gently rolled her onto her back, careful to keep his weight off her, and buried his face in her neck. The smell of her hair, the softness of her skin, the warmth of her under him; it was more pleasurable than he had imagined. She was holding him tight against her, her arms circling his shoulders and then passing down over the hard muscles in his back. She wrapped a leg around his hips, and there was no mistaking her desire or readiness for him.

He softly whispered her name as he shifted his position, making his intention clear, giving her one last chance to change her mind. She arched her back under him, moaning in pleasure, raising her hips in a motion of invitation. With one smooth, deliberate stroke, Acaraho claimed her as his own. He held his position for a moment, fully and deeply within her as they both savored the gratification of finally being one. He willed time to stop; for this never to end.

They moved together slowly at first, each lost in the other as the ecstasy built between them, relishing each moment, every movement, until they could hold back no longer. Finally—finally—their love for each other was satisfied as they both exploded in long-awaited release.

Their passion spent for the moment, Acaraho collapsed beside Adia. The two lay there together, gratified, content, and Acaraho drifted asleep.

He awoke the next morning and sat up with a start. He reached over on his sleeping mat, but Adia was not there. *Somehow, she must have left in the night after I fell asleep.* He could not remember anything past letting himself lie down next to her, the sweet smell of her beside him, and the pleasure of release spreading throughout his body, deeply relaxing him.

What are we to do now? What happens next? Acaraho asked himself. *What did it mean? Is she stepping down as Healer? Or was it just a lapse in her self-control, never to happen again?* He had to know what had caused her to come to him the night before. He had to find Adia.

In the Healer's Quarters, Adia was just waking up herself. It took her a moment before she remembered the previous night. She lay there for a long time, going over what had happened. She replayed every minute. It had been wonderful, everything she could have hoped. She knew it was not a dream. But she was confused, and she knew Acaraho would also be. She had to find him.

Adia rose and checked on Oh'Dar, who was still fast asleep. She smiled at him lovingly, touched at how he still slept with his bear. He was growing up, but there was still that little offspring in there somewhere, too.

As she was about to leave her quarters, Acaraho came down the corridor to her door. He stopped short when he saw her. She knew by his expression that he needed to speak with her as desperately as she needed to speak with him.

They looked at each other, and suddenly Adia felt shy. She looked down and then back up at Acaraho, fearing his judgment. He was standing in front of her, his eyes questioning. He reached out for her, and she went to him, taking his hand.

"We have to find somewhere private to talk," she said. At which he nodded, then turned to lead her to one of the empty rooms nearby.

Once inside, he turned and quickly took her in his arms and held her close. She started to protest, but it felt so wonderful to be pressed against his chest that she surrendered. He stroked her hair tenderly and sweetly. She was moved to tears by this expression of love. Acaraho was reassuring her that what had happened the previous night meant something to him as well—that it had not only been physical release. He was reminding her that he loved her.

She pulled away to look up at him, tears in her eyes.

"Adia," he said tenderly, his hand placed softly on her cheek, "Please do not cry, Saraste'. Please do not have any regrets. I could not bear it if you said you wish it had not happened."

His use of the endearment Saraste' touched Adia, but she shook her head. "Oh, Acaraho. My love. But it did not happen!"

"What are you saying? Of course it did. I remember every moment. Waking to see you standing there, how my heart pounded in anticipation as you came to me, how warm and soft you were, that kiss—and then—" his voice trailed off.

"I know. I know. But it was not real." *Oh, how do I make him understand when I barely understand it myself?* she thought.

"Adia, you cannot tell me it was a dream. That was no dream. That was real; what happened between us was as real as you and I are standing here now—" his confusion was growing.

Adia told him, "Remember Urilla Wuti? You know she has talents that many Healers do not have.

And you know that she taught me some of those. Well, what happened was not real. But it was not a dream either. Oh, I do not know how to explain it!" she said, her alarm growing that she had no idea how to make him understand.

She tried again. "My love. Think about it. How did I get into the room? How did I move your stone door, one of the largest there is—one you put there specifically to give you warning if someone tries to gain entry? How could I possibly have moved that door at all, let alone without you hearing it scraping along the floor, little by little?

"No matter how tired you might have been, you know you would have heard it!" she continued. "And you would have woken immediately."

He knew she was right. No matter how tired Acaraho was, some part of him was always on alert. And he had set the door just as she said—as a warning system should anyone try to enter while he was sleeping. There was probably no way she *could* have gotten the door open, let alone walked through it without him knowing.

"Are you saying that last night did not happen? Because I cannot accept that," he said.

"It is hard to explain. Perhaps it is better if I show you. But I must have your permission to do so. And it will mean that you will know me better than you ever thought possible, and I, in return, will know you. Are you willing to have all the veils stripped away between us?"

"I have no secrets from you, Adia. You have my permission to do whatever you want with me," he smiled, toying with her over last night's pleasure.

She lowered her eyes again, almost blushing. It was a lover's joke, and she relished that they might share that kind of intimate playfulness together as paired couples did.

She led him over to a seating area where they could face each other as Urilla Wuti had taught her. She took his hands in hers and prepared herself for the Connection. She wanted to keep it as light as she could because she knew the onslaught of experiences that could pass between them. If possible, she did not want him experiencing Khon'Tor's attack on her.

When she was ready, she opened her eyes and looked into Acaraho's. And then the Connection opened between them: Adia the Healer of the People of the High Rocks and Acaraho, their High Protector.

In that moment, time dropped out of existence, and the space separating Adia and Acaraho disappeared. The window between them opened. The consciousness of each merged with that of the other until there was only one, no longer separated but joined, knowing each other's hearts and minds in a way beyond explanation. Then, too soon, the process reversed, and they slowly separated, each becoming an individual again.

Adia had tried to keep it as shallow and brief as possible. She hoped she had succeeded, but, from the look on his face and from her own experience, knew she had failed.

Acaraho put his palm to his forehead, trying to collect himself. In that brief exchange, he had indeed merged deeper with Adia than she had intended. Perhaps it was the strong bond they already had that caused her to fail to keep it shallow. No matter how it happened and despite Adia's intentions, Acaraho had relived every moment of every painful experience in her life—including Khon'Tor's attack on her.

Acaraho now understood from the inside out Adia's reasoning for not turning in Khon'Tor. Like her, he remembered the pain at losing her father, her shame in front of the High Council. He experienced her grief at giving up Nimida and how she struggled not to think about her daughter. And he felt her deep, abiding love for him. It was like being two people at the same time, and his mind was reeling from its intensity.

He stood up and walked over to the far wall, still trying to come out of the swirling mass of feelings he was almost drowning in. He put a hand up and leaned against the cold surface. Where did he start and she begin?

If he had thought he hated Khon'Tor before, it was not even close to what he was feeling now.

And if he had thought he loved Adia before,

those feelings were not anywhere close to what he was feeling now, either.

"Acaraho, I am sorry. Perhaps I should have prepared you better; please forgive me!" She jumped up and went over to him, reaching up to place her hands on his shoulders.

He turned and took each of her hands in his. He pulled them both up to his chest and looked at her.

"Adia, I had no idea what you have been through; it is I who must apologize to you. I do not know how you have done it, living with all that every day. Yet still caring for others as you do," he said.

"I do not know why that Connection was so strong. I have some control over it, and I meant to keep it shallow and more contained," Adia tried to clarify.

"Will you explain to me what you just did and how you did it?" he asked, leading her back to the seating area.

Adia pulled herself together and started, "It's called a Connection. I do not know how many Healers can perform it. I learned it from Urilla Wuti. Before that, I had no idea such a thing was possible. There are multiple levels; each goes deeper and deeper. I made only the lightest Connection with you; I cannot explain why it was so strong. Perhaps because we are already connected. That is all I can think."

"If that was a shallow Connection, what are the deeper Connections like?" he asked.

"Each level is more and more invasive. If you go too deep, you can lose yourself in the other. The joining becomes intoxicating. And usually, after a Connection has been made, both need rest and time alone to process what they experienced. When we exchange experiences, we do not watch them from outside; we go through them just as the other did. And they leave a mark on us in exactly the same way."

She continued to explain to Acaraho what she could. She told him that a Connection should never be made with an offspring because they were unable to tolerate what most adults had endured.

Acaraho listened intently, never taking his eyes off her. He understood what she was saying about needing time to recover. He was in no state to go about his day-to-day business.

When she finished, he said, "So you think that what happened between us last night was some variation of this?"

"Yes. I believe it was. That is the only possible explanation. Somehow it was my mind's way of solving our dilemma. Wanting to be with you and not being able to. But I did not know it was possible, and even if I had, I would not have believed it could be so real. It also took me a moment to realize it was not!"

"It is hard to accept that it was not real. I can still feel you pressed up against me. I can feel your warm breath against my neck." he said, frowning.

Adia did blush then. "Acaraho." She shook her head. He could see she was trying to find delicate words to explain.

"For one thing, I have no memory of walking to your quarters, and I could hardly have moved the stone, let alone done it without waking you, but beyond that—of course, my first thought was the fear of being seeded. So I checked—" and she stopped then, knowing he could fill in the rest.

"Oh," was all Acaraho said, realizing for himself what she said was true; there was no mingled physical evidence that it had happened.

His hand rubbed his mouth as he mulled it over. Then he looked at Adia, and they both had the same thought at the same time.

"*This is wonderful!*" And they both laughed.

"Adia! Can you do this at will?" Acaraho asked, excited. *If this is true, then we can be with each other with no repercussions.* This was the answer to their frustrations and their dilemma—not able to move forward and unable to go back.

Adia put her hand to her mouth at their mutual realization, then exclaimed, "I do not know! I did not know it was even possible before last night! I hope so. I will ask Urilla Wuti!" she said, her voice lilting with happiness.

"How will you ask her? When can you ask her?"

"There are several ways. Once you are connected, you can exchange impressions over distances. Do you remember when you had the vision of where

Hakani and I were when she kidnapped Nootau? You told me that you saw in your mind the exact spot where we were standing."

Acaraho nodded.

"That was Urilla Wuti; she pushed that vision to you. But for this, I will need to establish a Connection with her as I just did with you. But it will take me a while to recover my strength."

Acaraho had a lot to think about. It was still early, and fortunately, he had time to go back to his quarters and process the experience.

"Find me after you talk to her," he said. Then he kissed her forehead and got up to leave.

"I am going to stay for a little while."

He nodded his understanding and left her to rest.

Adia took her time collecting herself. She knew Acaraho had a strong personality, but experiencing it herself had taken her by surprise. She was right in what she had believed all along. Acaraho was every bit as strong as Khon'Tor, except that he did not possess the all-encompassing drive for power that their Leader did.

She was struck with how much self-control he had. She had experienced for herself the strain he was under each day—from trying to manage his desire for her to suppressing his urge to make Khon'Tor pay for what he had done. However much respect she had for him before was now multiplied. Though, for some reason, she could not experience the other details of his life, she knew it had not been easy.

Adia was anxious to contact Urilla Wuti, but she could not manage it immediately. Besides, with Acaraho's feelings and experiences still fresh in her consciousness, it would be impossible not to share those with another person—even Urilla Wuti. She would have to practice partitioning some more; the ability to close off experiences shared by one in order not to share them with another. And there was also the matter of Urilla Wuti's memories. If she wished to connect deeper with Acaraho, she would have to partition what she had experienced of Urilla Wuti's life. She had a lot of work to do.

So Adia spent the rest of that morning alone, sorting out and recovering from her connection with Acaraho.

Acaraho made it back to his quarters and put the massive stone door back in place. He had to admit that there was no way Adia could have opened it by herself, and without making a sound.

He paced around his room. Physical activity helped him think, but he was not in a position to face other people. Adia's past experiences were still clear in his mind. He could feel the blow Khon'Tor had delivered to her head. He felt the fall to the cold, hard ground. And he experienced Khon'Tor's violation of her—though in her delirium all had not fully registered. And for that, he was thankful.

Oddly enough, he also experienced her desire for him. And mixed in with everything else was her experience of the past night. He was simultaneously experiencing the night before as himself and as her; he was at once the lover and the beloved.

Acaraho understood how someone could get lost in this. *And what would a deeper Connection be like?* Putting that thought out of his mind and finally finding some humor, he chuckled to himself, *Well, now I know the answer to the age-old question males have been pondering for generations regarding whose splendor lasts longer. And it is definitely that of the female.*

Urilla Wuti was sitting in meditation when she felt Adia reach out to her. She immediately understood the young Healer's question without the need for words. And she answered in return, explaining what had happened.

It was as Adia had suspected. Their long, unfulfilled desire for each other, coupled with her desperation for a solution, had allowed her to open a Connection with Acaraho in the Dream World. In this case, she was somehow able to project herself into his room as a full-bodied manifestation of her consciousness. And yes, she could do this at will, but she would need to practice it just as she did with any new skill.

Urilla Wuti offered to work with her on this new-found ability. The older Healer was pleased to see that her years of training Adia were coming together. Far more was possible than that which Adia had accidentally discovered the night before. Urilla Wuti would explain it to her in time, but Adia had to learn to walk before she could run.

Oh'Dar woke to find his mother already gone. He propped his bear back up in its spot to the side of his sleeping mat. He was anxious to get to his workshop. He had an idea of something to make for Honovi and enjoyed imagining her pleasure when he presented her with it. For the first time in a long time, he was happy again, and for the moment, was not troubled by his usual feelings of displacement. Having his own workroom made him feel useful and gave him a new sense of belonging.

Oh'Dar had made a mental list during his time with the Brothers. He enjoyed seeing his inventions in use around Kthama. Though subtle, his improvements made all their lives easier.

But before he could get to work, he had to take Kweeuu outside. When he was ready, Oh'Dar picked up the cub and padded down the corridor and out through the Great Entrance.

He took Kweeuu to the spot he had chosen for the wolf cub to use. It was fairly close to the entrance, yet out of the way of foot traffic. He wanted Kweeuu eventually to go out by himself and did not want the area to be so far away that the cub might be tempted to wander off.

When the cub was finished, Oh'Dar called him, and Kweeuu followed his master back inside. Oh'Dar took a moment to look up at the clear blue sky directly above. Soft, dark winter clouds were moving in. The cold weather was coming, but he did not mind; he had new wrappings to try out.

On the way back, they stopped at the eating area to pick up the scraps that the older females had started collecting for Kweeuu.

Khon'Tor was having his breakfast when Oh'Dar entered the Great Chamber. Though Khon'Tor knew that he could do nothing about the boy's presence, he was still convinced that it would bring trouble to the People. Possibly the Waschini offspring would even cause an inevitable onset of Wrak-Ayya, the Age of Shadows.

Akule approached Khon'Tor and asked to sit with him. Khon'Tor nodded; he had still not decided what to do with Akule, but for now, found him useful.

The watcher sat down across from Khon'Tor and turned around to see what had caught the Leader's attention. He saw Oh'Dar waiting at the meal preparation area.

"The boy is growing; he is a young man already," offered Akule, trying to start a conversation.

"Yes, he is. In a few years, he will be old enough to mate. I have often wondered what will become of him then," Khon'Tor replied. "If we are lucky, he will take a mate from the Brothers and become their problem," he continued.

"I thought you had accepted him," said Akule, then immediately regretted it; Khon'Tor might see that as a challenge.

"I accept that Oh'Dar is here, Akule. But I still do not like it," said Khon'Tor, a bit too loudly.

"He has family somewhere. And no matter how poorly we think of the Waschini, *someone* must be looking for him. It is just a matter of time before he brings disaster to our community. I am convinced it will be he who brings the Age of Shadows down on all our heads," said Khon'Tor.

"We already had one close call when he and the Whitespeak teacher were almost discovered by the Waschini riders this spring. Mark my words, that Waschini will be the downfall of all of us. And when that happens, the blame will land squarely on the Healer's shoulders," he finished.

Khon'Tor abruptly shoved what was left of his meal away from him and rose to leave.

As the Leader turned, he noticed Oh'Dar standing there. Instead of trying to repair the damage, he turned to Akule and said, "You wanted to talk to me about something? If so, then walk with me." And he headed for the exit.

On the way back inside, Oh'Dar stopped at the eating area to pick up the scraps that the older females had started collecting for Kweeuu. While they were waiting, Kweeuu took off to beg for food from the tables. Oh'Dar chased after the little cub and scooped him up in his arms. Then Khon'Tor mentioned his name, and he paused. He stood frozen, a few feet away from the two males.

Oh'Dar heard everything the Leader said; *that he would be the ruin of everyone there. It would be his fault that the People would suffer. And his mother would take the blame.*

Khon'Tor's words cut him to the quick.

Oh'Dar walked blankly back to collect the scraps from the females, thanked them, and hurried back to his workshop with Kweeuu. He closed the door behind them, thankful for a place of his own where he could deal with his feelings in private.

Adult males were not supposed to cry, but Oh'Dar was not yet fully an adult. He still sometimes felt very young, despite being only a few years from pairing age.

He dropped the scraps for Kweeuu, who readily scarfed them up, then sank down on the nearest stack of furs. Burying his face in his hands, Oh'Dar let the tears flow. How he wished he was young enough for his mother or Nadiwani to be there to hold him.

As bad as Oh'Dar had felt before, at least he knew he had a home with the People. Now he did not know where to go. He could go to the Brothers, but Adia and Acaraho would come and get him. He could not tell them what he had overheard. He knew they would be furious to learn what Khon'Tor had said about him.

"*Someone is looking for him.*" "*He has family somewhere.*" The words echoed in his mind. Oh'Dar wondered if it could be true. Was there a Waschini family somewhere wondering what had become of him? Odd that it had never occurred to him before.

I wonder if I could find them? And would they want me back? I need to ask mother again about how she found me. Maybe there is a clue somewhere to help me find my Waschini family.

For the first time, Oh'Dar realized how much he loved this family. He did not want to leave them. But he would not be the cause for any harm coming to them either.

Oh'Dar did not get any work done that day. He stayed in his workshop, nursing his wounds and absent-mindedly teaching Kweeuu new tricks.

If, as she had with Nootau and Nimida, Urilla Wuti had established a Connection for Adia with Oh'Dar, the Healer would have known the boy was in distress. But Urilla Wuti had not, and her distraction over Acaraho was occupying her mind. Strong emotions always dampened the seventh sense.

Akule and Khon'Tor had walked to the Great Entrance to talk. Standing in the middle of the cave, all was silent except for the drip of water from condensation on the stalactites above.

"Khon'Tor, I am thinking of asking to be paired. Do you know when the High Council will be considering pairings again?"

Khon'Tor was surprised. He had not thought about whether Akule was paired or not.

"It has been a long time since the last decent-sized pairing ceremony. I will find out." Khon'Tor was again thinking about his own situation.

"Thank you, Adik'Tor." And Akule left to take his shift as watcher.

The Leader sat down on one of the seating stones along the perimeter. There had not been a full-scale Ashwea Awhidi since Adia rescued Oh'Dar.

Khon'Tor decided it was time to select a mate. When he sent word to the High Council on Akule's behalf, he decided he would also ask about the youngest females available for his consideration.

He needed an heir, and besides, it felt like a lifetime since he had enjoyed himself with Hakani. Just thinking about it started his pulse racing. Only his fear of exposure had held his drive in check all these years. He steeled his thoughts against remembering the sheer pleasure of taking a female despite her protestations—so easily overpowering her, forcing himself inside her, taking what he wanted—the satisfaction of her soft flesh yielding to his assault.

Yes, it has been too long.

Adia was excited to give Acaraho the news that she could learn to create the same third-dimensional Connection they had experienced the night before. And once she learned how to do this, she and Acaraho could share whatever experiences they wished with no real-world repercussions.

Once again, the Great Mother had answered, providing a solution to their suffering that neither could ever have imagined.

As Adia was about to go and find Acaraho, Nadiwani came to find her. The Helper entered the room, took one look at Adia, and stopped short.

"What have you done?" she blurted out. "What have you done, Adia?" She repeated the question, this time as if Adia knew full well what she had done.

"I do not know what you are talking about!" Adia looked at Nadiwani, her brows knitted together in genuine confusion.

Then Adia remembered that Nadiwani also possessed a relatively well-developed seventh sense, even if it was not strong enough for her to be a Healer. *Uh-oh.*

Nadiwani stood with her arms crossed over her chest and looked at Adia disapprovingly.

"It is not what you think," answered Adia. "And I cannot explain it right now, but I hope I can someday!" Urilla Wuti had not given her permission to tell Nadiwani about the Connection.

"Alright, Adia. Say what you will. But be careful," said Nadiwani.

Despite Adia's denial, Nadiwani was convinced that Acaraho and Adia had mated.

Despite Adia's protestations, Nadiwani still thought it likely that Acaraho was the sire of Nootau and Nimida, as much as she wanted to believe the contrary. If it were true, then on one level, Nadiwani was glad they had finally given in. She could see how much they loved each other, and she hated to see them suffer as they did. But she also knew that Adia was devoted to her position as Healer. If things continued, Adia would have to step down.

Now that they had started down that road, Nadiwani could only pray that Adia would henceforth take successful precautions to avoid being seeded again.

Khon'Tor sent word to the High Council Overseer inquiring about the next full celebration of pairings. Kurak'Kahn sent a reply that it would be three springs hence.

Khon'Tor decided to make a general announcement telling the parents to consider which of their offspring would be of age and would be interested in being paired, and asking the singles to give thought to their situations. For his purposes, he must talk to the Leaders of each of the Communities to learn who would be available for pairing. Khon'Tor was confident that any of his peers would be thrilled should one of their females be paired with the great Leader of the People of the High Rocks.

Word of the general assembly spread very quickly, and the community was humming with speculation about the possible reasons for it.

Adia found Acaraho leaving a meeting with the guards and watchers. He signed to her to join him as he walked away from the group. She stepped in line with him and waited until they were out of earshot before speaking.

"I connected with Urilla Wuti. Yes, I can learn how to re-create last night. Well," Adia said, blushing, "Not *last night exactly,* but the experience of being together while still in the Dream World," she explained.

Acaraho listened intently as they walked along, occasionally glancing over at her as they talked. He tried to focus, but his thoughts kept going back to the night before. That they could experience being together like that again, as real as it felt, started his heart pounding.

"Forgive my eagerness, Adia," he said, smiling. "But when do your lessons start?" and he laughed joyously.

She laughed with him.

"I have never been so anxious to turn in as I will be tonight," he teased her, reading her mind. He knew he was making her blush, and that pleased him no end. He loved his effect on her, and hers on him.

From now on, the nighttime farewell, "Sweet Dreams," would carry a special meaning for both of them.

Later, Adia realized she had not seen Oh'Dar all day. She decided he must be in his workshop. Not wanting to be an overbearing mother, she resisted the inclination to check in on him. However, if he did not show up at mealtime, she would risk it anyway. No matter how excited he was about his projects, he still had to eat.

Mealtime came, and Oh'Dar showed up as expected. The five of them sat together; Adia, Nootau, Nadiwani, Oh'Dar, and Acaraho. Not too long after, Mapiya, Haiwee, and Pakuna joined them.

"What do you think the general assembly is about?" asked Mapiya. Given their rank, she thought that Adia or Acaraho might know.

"I have no clue," answered Adia. Acaraho said that he did not either.

"Well, at least it is nothing to worry about then," observed Haiwee. She was right; if there were trouble, one of them, and probably both, would already know of it.

Adia noticed that Oh'Dar was picking at his food.

Her heart sank. *Oh no*, she thought. *Please do not let this start up again. And he was so happy just yesterday!*

Kweeuu scampered around joyfully from table to table, charming scraps from each person there. Adia noticed and mentioned it to Oh'Dar.

"That cub is going to be as fat as a log. Perhaps you should keep him back in our room during mealtimes?" she suggested, trying to draw him out.

"Alright, Mama. I will. Do you think we could spend some time together tonight, just you and I?" he asked tentatively.

"Well, of course," she replied. Oh'Dar had never asked this before, so she was both happy and concerned. "I will be sure to get back to our quarters early."

Her earlier distraction with Acaraho cleared as

she realized her son was again struggling with something.

Adia made sure she did as she had said. She was back in time to ensure that, if need be, they would have the whole evening together.

Adia walked into the Healer's Quarters to find Oh'Dar on his sleeping mat, playing with Kweeuu. She noticed he had put his bear up on a higher ledge, presumably because Kweeuu had tried to claim it as his own.

"I see that your bear is now in a safer place," she remarked.

"Yes, Kweeuu got hold of him earlier and was about to tear him up. I am thinking of making Kweeuu something similar to play with from one of the skins," he replied.

"What a great idea. I am sure he will love that. And perhaps it will keep him out of everything else," Adia said, smiling as she went over and sat down next to Oh'Dar. As she did, he leaned over and fell into her arms. She cradled him as she had when he was a little boy, relishing that he still needed her, even while her heart was breaking that he was so sad.

"Mama," he said, his nose buried in her neck. "Would you tell me again how you found me? Only, this time, go slowly and do not leave anything out," he asked.

"Of course, Oh'Dar. I will try to remember everything," she said, leaning back against the wall so they could sit more comfortably.

Once settled, she began.

"It was nearly Fall. I was preparing to take a satchel of Goldenseal roots to Ithua. It had been an excellent harvest, and the plants take five to seven cycles to mature. I knew she could use them—any Healer could. I set out in the morning, planning to be back by twilight. Nadiwani was worried that I was going while Khon'Tor was away at a High Council meeting, but I felt compelled to.

"The waters of the river were high where I usually crossed it, so I was forced to take a longer route. It was a beautiful morning, and the air was filled with birdsong and the sweet fragrance of the late-blooming flowers," she continued.

"As I came to a clearing, I saw a wooden construction in the distance with two horses still tied to it. Honovi later told me it is called a wagon. I knew something was wrong, so I approached. I unlashed the horses, and they took off in opposite directions. There were two Waschini people there who had returned to the Mother. Whoever killed them tried to make it look like the work of the Brothers."

She stopped.

"Go on, Mama, do not worry. I did not know them; it will not hurt me," he lied. Adia wanted to do as he said, but there were certain details about his parents' slaughter that she would never tell him.

"Alright. It was clear they had not died naturally. I said a prayer for them, and as I was turning to go, I heard something. It was your sweet little voice coming from inside the wagon. However those who harmed the couple did not discover you, I do not know. When I moved the covers, you were lying there looking up at me, grinning away, your beautiful sky blue eyes smiling. I knew I could not leave you, so I gathered you up and brought you back inside the Goldenseal satchel. There were a couple of items with you, and your bear, which you still have. The other items I put away for someday when you were older and would be able to take care of them," she finished.

"What were the other items? I do not remember you telling me that part before," his voice filled with excitement.

"One was a little blanket that was with you in your sleeping box. It was the same color as your eyes and embellished with some type of stitching. The other was a locket."

"A locket?" he asked.

"Yes. I will get them for you if you want. You are old enough to take care of them now," said Adia.

Much as she hated to stand up and have him stop cuddling with her, Adia got up and retrieved the blanket and locket. Many years before, she had put them out of the way of his little inquisitive hands for safekeeping.

Is'Taqa had returned the locket, explaining that Acaraho had handed it to him the night they rescued her after Khon'Tor's attack. Adia had thought for sure it was lost, and she cried tears of joy when she saw it, though it saddened her that the little pouch had been destroyed. The last she remembered of it was Khon'Tor ripping the pouch open with his teeth and tossing it to the treetops below. Then he had held the locket up in front of her face and shouted at her just before he hit her.

Adia sat down next to Oh'Dar once more. She first handed him the soft little blanket. He rubbed it against his face before turning it over to look at the embroidery.

After he had looked the blanket over, she told him to put his hand out, and she placed the locket in his open palm. She showed him how to open it and pointed out the two pictures inside.

"I do not know how it was created, but those are images of your mother and father, Oh'Dar," she explained.

Oh'Dar peered at the little pictures and looked up at Adia.

"You are my mother, and Acaraho is my father." He stared at the locket for a long time.

Adia spoke once more. "Please find a safe place for them, out of sight. Khon'Tor was not pleased with me for bringing them back with you. He was afraid that the locket could identify you." She hesitated to say that but felt she needed to give some explanation.

Oh'Dar said he would and hugged his mother again. They sat together and spoke of other things.

When they had stopped talking, and Oh'Dar was alone again, he picked up the locket. He raised it as close to his eyes as he could focus. He had never seen anything like it. He could not identify the stone it was made from—it was hard and shiny, and did not really appear to be stone at all.

He thought he could see the same light eyes in each of the images. The woman had dark curly hair. The man had the same straight dark hair as his. The wrappings they wore were foreign to him. In the back of his mind, Oh'Dar was thinking that these were the clues he had been hoping to find.

Later, Oh'Dar did as his mother had said and found a safe place for the locket and the blanket. He planned to spend the rest of the cold indoor season fashioning himself wrappings that did not resemble the Brothers' style at all. He was setting his plans in motion, and he wanted no repercussions for the Brothers.

The next two days passed, and it was time. Happy with anticipation, everyone arrived ahead of the assembly horn. Acaraho and Adia also looked forward to the meeting, having no concerns about whatever the announcement would be.

As usual, everyone became quiet when Khon'Tor walked to the front of the room and raised his hand to speak.

"Thank you for coming. Please be sure to spread the word to anyone not in attendance this afternoon. It has been many years since the last full Ashwea Awhidi. As you remember, all those since included far fewer pairings. However, the High Council Overseer has informed me that the High Council will be accepting pairing requests for a large-scale ceremony.

"Parents, you should consider which of your offspring might be ready to be paired. Unpaired adults, please also consider your situations. I will be sending initial word back to the High Council by the time the forsythia bloom, so please let me know if you are interested.

"The High Council will be holding the Ashwea Awhidi three springs hence. Carefully consider this opportunity since we do not know how soon another may be offered. That is all." And with that, he dropped his hand, signaling he was done.

The room filled with happy conversation. Akule was standing at the back, already wondering with whom he might be paired. He had been a bachelor for so long, but it was time. He longed to have a family of his own. It was seeing how happy Acaraho and Adia were that had led him to reconsider his single status.

Adia saw Nootau looking over questioningly at her—by that time, he would be old enough to be paired—but she ignored him. Nootau was only a little over a year younger than Oh'Dar, but from what Adia could tell, the Washini seemed to mature later than the People. She could see that Nootau would be ready to take a mate by the time of this next Ashwea Awhidi.

Acaraho looked over at Nootau and winked at him. The young male understood that his mother did not welcome the thought that he was growing up, and he grinned back at Acaraho.

Nootau might have inherited his father's build, but he had not inherited his father's personality. Where Khon'Tor was driven, aggressive, self-centered, Nootau was amiable, kind, and generous. It was a shame that his relationship to Khon'Tor would never be known; Nootau would have made a great Leader.

Lost in the happy mood, someone blurted out to Khon'Tor as he walked by, "What about you, Khon'-Tor? Is it not time you took another mate?"

Everyone stopped to hear his answer. All the available females waited in suspense.

"You are right, Kachina," he replied, addressing

the female who was brave enough to ask what all the others were wondering.

"It is past due that I take another mate. I am considering it," he said.

Everyone was happy to hear that, and it added to the celebratory mood. Nearly everyone remained in the Great Chamber for quite some time, enjoying the exciting announcement and discussing who would be entered for pairing.

Adia was glad to hear this. Life needed to move on, even for Khon'Tor. However, after Hakani's allegations regarding his mating appetites, she would be keeping a close eye on him.

CHAPTER 4

The community was abuzz for days over Khon'Tor's announcement. Though the High Council decided most pairings, occasionally a couple would fall in love and ask to be paired. Those requests also had to be submitted to the High Council, members of which carefully reviewed each one with an eye to the genetic diversity of the population. The dark period between the Brothers and the People was never to be repeated.

Acaraho and Adia later discussed Nootau's readiness to be paired and decided they would put the question to him. Adia could not yet see her son as a fully grown male, and he did not seem old enough to either of them, but Acaraho reminded her that the pairing was still a fair while in the future.

As for Oh'Dar, Adia felt there was no question of it at all. Even though there was still time before the event, she could not see Oh'Dar being mature

enough to take on the responsibilities of a life partner. Besides, Oh'Dar had his current problems to
worry about. Adia hoped that his good mood would
return as he continued working with his skins and
hides.

In some ways, Adia got her wish as Oh'Dar
engrossed himself in his sewing. He also worked on
the gift he had in mind for Honovi and decided to
make one for Is'Taqa and each of their daughters as
well. He planned on making little fur booties for
Noshoba, their little son.

Adia's relief at seeing Oh'Dar so busy in his workshop every day was ill-founded. She had recently
become very cautious about using her seventh sense
with her sons. She knew she had to be careful to
keep concealed the fact that Nootau's father was
Khon'Tor, not Acaraho. Had she known what Oh'Dar
was planning, she would have been beside herself
with fear.

Oh'Dar did not want to think about being paired.
He knew there was not a mate for him among the
People. And he had too much to accomplish to think
of entering the grown-up world of responsibilities
and offspring.

The only thing on his mind right now was Khon'-
Tor's statement. That he was a threat to everyone he
loved.

Kweeuu's vocabulary had grown considerably. Though Oh'Dar had focused more on teaching him Handspeak words, Kweeuu also responded to voice commands. Much to the delight of the offspring, Oh'Dar had also taught him *speak, no-speak, bring back, find,* and to spin while standing up on his back legs. Oh'Dar had also taught the cub not to beg from anyone in the eating room. Oh'Dar knew that if he did not nip that in the bud, his mother would ban Kweeuu from the community areas.

Though Oh'Dar still thought of him as a cub, Kweeuu was growing alongside his master. The wolf was halfway to his full size, and his beautiful, thick, grey coat was starting to come in. He was going to be large, and Oh'Dar knew it was vital that he be taught good manners. Soon it would be impossible to pick up his pet and carry him away from trouble.

To their disappointment, no more midnight visits materialized for Adia and Acaraho. They tried to be patient and savored their memory of that one time they'd had together.

Adia's work with Urilla Wuti continued. Entering the Dream World at will was a different skill than connecting with another person. She had to reach into the abyss, trying to access another reality with no destination consciousness to find. It was like walking in the dark blindfolded with her hands stretched out before her.

Adia often returned to the secluded little cave with the clear shallow waters that she had been coming to for years now. It was her place of solace, and it provided the peace and privacy she needed to practice. Alone in the cozy chamber, she was free of distractions. So, one morning, when all her tasks were caught up, and there were no more pressing issues, she took time to slip away and try again.

She sat in the little alcove, safe and secluded, and shifted her weight until she was comfortable and safely propped up in place. She quieted her mind to enter a state of meditation. This time, as her mind became clearer and clearer, she felt an opening. It was similar to the window that appeared when making a Connection, only it was not as well-defined. It was softer and larger. As she continued to quiet her consciousness, allowing instead of forcing, she felt as if she were physically stepping through a portal.

She opened her eyes to see a world more beautiful than could be imagined. It was very much like Etera, only everything was richer. The colors were more vibrant. The sky was a deeper blue. She could hear birdsong, except it was more than birdsong. She seemed to have senses she had never experienced before. There were no words adequate to describe it.

Adia was standing in a clearing under a canopy of trees. Sunlight broke through, creating a dappled pattern on the carpet of grass beneath her feet. Wild-flowers encircled the perimeter of the glade. In the distance, she could see what looked very much like the high rocks surrounding Kthama. It was familiar and yet not familiar. She looked down at her hands. She still had her physical body. She could feel the ground supporting her weight. She ran her fingers over her arms—everything felt the same but sweeter, gentler, clearer.

She quieted her mind further, allowing herself to open to whatever else there was to perceive. Suddenly, reality shifted again, and she could feel a Presence. If it had been a sound, it would have been an ever-present hum, light and airy and pleasant. If it had been a color, it would have been the most vibrant color imaginable. If it had been tangible, it would have been soft and strong yet yielding and enveloping in the most comforting way possible. As for an emotion—it was clearly love.

Adia could feel how everything was being thought into existence by the Great Mind, held in its existence through the intention of the Great Will, and protected and guided by the binding force of the love of the Great Heart. She had been taught about the three aspects of the Great Spirit, The One-Who-is-Three and The Three-Who-Are-One, but now she felt she was only beginning to understand for the first time how they worked together. It was as if everything had consciousness; the colors, the sounds, the textures—even the light.

She did not want to leave this place. She did not want to leave this Presence. She fleetingly wondered what was beyond the glade, and somehow knew there was so much more in this place—so much more to come.

From a distance, a figure was approaching unhurriedly. Adia could tell it was a female. A female who was familiar and meant her no harm. As the figure came closer, she recognized a much younger Urilla Wuti! Adia clasped her hands in joy while wondering how her mentor's youthful appearance was possible.

"Urilla!" Adia exclaimed, then caught herself, realizing she had inadvertently used the familiar form of her mentor's name.

"Adia. What do you think?" The female approached and took Adia's hands in hers, just as she always did.

"Of this place? Of here? Oh, it's beyond anything I could ever have imagined. *But where are we?*" she asked.

"It is hard to explain. The short answer is that this is where we go after we leave Etera."

"Do you mean we are dead? Have we returned to the Mother?" Alarm was in Adia's voice. She was not ready to leave Nootau, Oh'Dar, or Acaraho!

"No, Adia. This is where we come when we leave our bodies in death, yes. But you and I have not returned to the Mother. This place—this is more like a connector. It is called the Corridor. You and I can come and go, and we can use it to meet as now, to further your training," she explained.

"How did you know I was here?" Adia asked, trying to select the most important of the hundreds of questions swirling in her head.

"I felt you enter. You have done well—and in such a short time. I know it may not seem like it considering all the years we have been training, but not many make it to this level."

"Where are our real selves while we are here?" asked Adia, assuming she was still in the little cave with only her thoughts projected to this place.

"My real self is here. With you, right now, just as your real self is here with me right now. Our world, Etera, the world we have left, is only a projection of this world. *This is reality;* the world we think we live in is only a pale echo of our true home," she explained.

Adia looked around and knew that what Urilla Wuti said was true. This *was* reality. This was far more real than anything she had ever experienced. She had it backward, thinking that she was imagining herself in this place. In fact, from this place, she was imagining herself in Etera. It was very confusing, but at the same time, it had the ring of truth.

"So, is this the Dream World?" she asked.

"No. This is the Corridor, not the Dream World, but you did have a Dream World experience with Acaraho that you wish to recreate. Which told me that you were ready for this step," said Urilla Wuti, her eyes twinkling.

"Well, yes, that is why I contacted you. I wanted to know how to create it again. Must I somehow bring Acaraho here?"

"Though the day may come when you are strong enough to bring him here, I would not attempt it, Adia. Remember how I explained that these Connections can become intoxicating and that the longer you stay in a deep Connection, the harder it can be to break it off? Well, here it is tenfold so."

Adia blushed, immediately understanding. *The experience of life was so intense there, richer, deeper—.*

"If this is not where we meet, then how?" Adia was not even sure how to ask it.

"Now that you have been here and experienced this place for yourself, your abilities will take another giant step forward. And each time you come to the Corridor, they will be enhanced again. When you return, you will find that if you set your intention before you drift off to sleep, you will be able to find Acaraho again in the Dream World, and it will be just as real as it was the first time."

"In all this grand design, it sounds so selfish now to want that." Adia lowered her eyes, embarrassed.

"Not at all, Adia. We were made to long for each other. The need to join together physically is no more selfish than the need to breathe or sleep or eat. Love draws us one to another; love joins with itself in the physical expression between the lover and the beloved. Just as when our bodies fail, love draws us home."

Urilla Wuti leaned forward and hugged Adia. "We should both be getting back," she said.

Adia did not want to leave and knew that she would return at the first opportunity. "Urilla Wuti, part of me does not want to go back. Could I not just stay? Or, if not, when I die, can I stay here? Do I have to return to the Mother?"

"You do not have to go back now, Adia. It is your choice, as it will be when you die. But if you stay now, back in the shadow world of Etera your body will eventually die. And, though you can choose to stay here now, or when you die, you will still want to return to the Mother at some point. This place is beautiful, but even it pales against our final return Home."

"I am not sure how I got here. How *do* I go back?"

"Close your eyes and surrender your will. Give up your desire to stay, and empty your consciousness. Then, create an intention to return. An intention is a movement of your soul, the part of the Great Will that lives through you."

Adia closed her eyes and tried to do as Urilla Wuti had said. She found her awareness of sitting in the little cave starting to return. As consciousness came back to her body, she slowly opened her eyes. She felt small. She felt like a washed-out version of herself. As beautiful as the little cave had been to her, it now seemed like an empty echo of reality.

She had left reality, not returned to it.

Adia had no idea how much time had passed. It felt like only a few minutes, but Urilla Wuti had once told her that time did not always behave as one expected in experiences like this.

Adia padded anxiously back to her quarters. Oh'Dar was not there, and she could see from the light filtering down over the worktable that it was daytime. She wanted to stay there to savor and revisit her experience, but she must know how long she had been gone. She chuckled at her dilemma. *How does one ask if today is still today*?

The only way she knew was to find someone else and see if they remarked that she had been missing for a while.

Luckily for Adia, there were several people in the Great Chamber. It appeared that it was mid-day because the morning meal had been cleared away. She spotted Nadiwani sitting at one of the tables and tried to approach nonchalantly.

The Helper waved her over, but not frantically, as she would if Adia had been missing for some time.

So far, so good.

"How has your morning been?" Nadiwani asked. Adia held back a huge sigh of relief.

"Well," she answered, "I think I am going to prepare some Ginseng powder this afternoon. We seem to have a great stockpile of roots."

"Do you want help?" asked Nadiwani.

Adia realized she had not spent much time with

her friend for quite a while and nodded her agreement. She hoped she was not going to get another scolding about Acaraho. What she wanted to do was find him and tell him about her experience this morning, but Nadiwani said that he and Nootau were out scouting for white cedar and locust trees for tool making.

That afternoon, Adia did her best to focus on the task at hand. She had forgotten how well she and Nadiwani worked together, and in no time, they had made a significant dent in the overstock of Ginseng roots. But she had a hard time shaking the feeling that this was all make-believe. She hoped that in time, the feeling would pass; this was the world she had to live in for now.

"Are you thinking about whether Nootau will be ready to take a mate in the next pairing?" asked Nadiwani.

Nadiwani is as close to being Nootau's mother as I am, so she shares my concern. It is time that she, Acaraho, and I sit down and discuss it.

"I think the three of us need to talk about it, and then afterward see how Nootau feels about it," Adia answered.

"Thank you. I realize that this is a decision for you and Acaraho to make."

"No, not really. You have raised Nootau and Oh'Dar as much as I have. We are an odd family, but we are a family just the same," she mused. She wrapped an arm around Nadiwani's shoulder and squeezed her close. "Speaking of Oh'Dar, it seems like forever since he came out of that workshop."

"He is spending a great deal of time in there, but he seems intent on his projects. I will stop by and bring him to the evening meal; how's that?" said Nadiwani.

"Great. I think I will clean up and then try to find Acaraho. There is something I want to tell him, and then the three of us can plan to meet about Nootau." Adia brushed together the leavings on her side of the worktable and dumped them in the discard basket.

As Adia started down the familiar corridor toward the Great Chamber, she idly watched her feet take one step after the other as she allowed her mind to clear. A small smile crossed her lips; she was anxious to tell Acaraho her good news. She slipped through the crowd and spotted him across the room. Not wanting to interrupt, she took a seat at one of the empty tables and waited for him to notice her.

It did not take long. Acaraho caught the attention of the male he had been speaking with and tilted his head in Adia's direction. The other male smiled and left to find his mate.

Perched on the edge of the seat, Adia found it hard not to fidget. Oh, so hard she tried not to watch him approach, but she failed miserably. Openly admiring him, her eyes passed over his form from head to toe as he walked toward her.

"You look like a female who is up to something," he teased her.

Her pulse quickened at his closeness as he straddled the bench to face her, his knees inches from hers.

"I may have good news," she said, a shy smile crossing her lips. She made him wait.

"You're killing me," he said, his eyes twinkling with devilish charm.

Adia laughed at his impatience. "I cannot promise anything, but I, for one, will be turning in early tonight."

Acaraho leaned forward, rubbed his mouth, and rested his chin on his hand as if thinking long and hard about something. He caught her gaze and then slowly looked her up and down before returning his eyes to hers. He raised an eyebrow, and a slightly sinister smile crossed his lips.

He's flirting with me! she thought. And their newfound lovers' play was delicious fun. *Oh, so this is how it's going to be!*

Before she could return the favor, Nadiwani showed up with the young males in tow. Adia was thrilled to see Oh'Dar after his long absence. They sat together as a family and enjoyed the evening meal.

"Mama, would you be upset if I set up a sleeping mat in my workshop? Sometimes I may want to work late, and I do not want to disturb you when I come home."

Adia was not ready for her first son to move out on his own but realized that was not what he was saying. He had always been a sweet boy, and no doubt, he was simply being considerate.

"If that is what you want, Oh'Dar. I am sure Mapiya or any of the others will be glad to help you with it."

"Thanks. I think I'll also make a little mat for Kweeuu!"

Adia laughed at the image of a matching wolf-sized sleeping mat next to Oh'Dar's. While he and Nadiwani continued discussing his new sleeping arrangement, Adia kept her expression neutral but slowly inched her leg over, and under the table, she pressed it up against Acaraho's.

He dropped his food.

The others stared at him.

Realizing that if this continued, he would be trapped sitting there for some time, Acaraho said he was going to retire early and got up to leave.

As he walked past Adia, he stopped directly beside her and pressed his leg against hers. He placed one hand on her shoulder. Then he leaned over and let his lips and warm breath lightly brush her ear as he whispered, 'Sweet Dreams."

Everything within Adia tightened deliciously in response. The evening could not pass quickly enough.

The rest talked among themselves as they finished their meal. Nootau asked if he could go and play with Kweeuu, and Oh'Dar agreed enthusiastically. He was anxious to show Nootau all the new tricks that the young wolf already knew.

Adia's mind bounced from topic to topic. She bit her lip to try and settle down. She pushed her food around but did not eat. From across the table, Nadiwani threw a mushroom cap at her to get her attention.

Adia jumped and glared at her friend.

"Goodness! You two have to tone it down!" Nadiwani's hands flashed quickly, not wanting the boys to see.

Adia did not want to tone it down. If anything, she wanted to stoke it up, at least to forest blaze proportions. But Nadiwani's point was well made. They were acting openly like a paired couple. So far, Adia and Acaraho had support and acceptance of their arrangement from the majority of the community. But there were still a few who looked at them askance.

Both Adia and Acaraho were kind and humble, wholeheartedly giving of themselves to the community. Adia spent countless hours at the bedsides of those who needed her services. Those who reported to Acaraho respected and looked up to him without reservation. Had Adia and Acaraho been different people, the community might well have turned against them long ago.

But it was still not acceptable protocol for the Healer to have an offspring—let alone to be raising two. Adia had broken a Second Law by allowing herself to be seeded. Everyone thought Acaraho was Nootau's father, and to flaunt their relationship openly was asking for trouble.

Change was hard for the People, and Adia was lucky that things were going this well. Nadiwani was wise to warn her that she had better not push the line too far, and Adia knew it. So she nodded at her friend. *Message received.*

Acaraho greeted several of the guards on his way through the hall. He made a point of stopping at the table of the unpaired males to chide them good-naturedly.

"I was glad to hear of Khon'Tor's announcement. I am sure you will have a lot on your minds over the upcoming months," he said.

The round of males chuckled and nodded.

Akule volunteered, "I know I will!" He brought his palm down on the table with a bang for emphasis. The males broke out in laughter, and those on either side of him clapped the watcher on his back and grinned knowingly. Akule enjoyed the good-natured kidding of his peers. He had watched other couples for some time, and he saw the goodwill and kindness between them. He hoped the same rewarding experience awaited him.

Most of the males abandoned their single status within several years, if not months, of becoming eligible. Others, like Akule, struggled with the decision for some time. Usually, those who wanted to live with their mate took longer to decide because it was such a life-changing decision.

The High Council took great care to match pairs who had the same goals. In Akule's case, as someone who wanted a true partner to create a family pod, the High Council would not select a mate for him that round if there was not a female with the same goal.

Not everyone who was paired would establish a family. For many of them, it was a means to an end. As a result, there were couples who came together only for enjoyment and procreation, returning afterward to their separate lifestyles.

Sometimes, once the offspring came, the pair moved into private quarters as a family unit. But it was not unusual for a mother and father to raise their offspring without ever building a life together as a family.

The unpaired males often lived together for support and companionship. Unpaired females, however, usually stayed with their family, close to their mothers.

It was still early when Acaraho got to his quarters. He paced around the room, thoughts whirling.

He absent-mindedly straightened his sleeping mat and tidied the items on his worktable. Then he leaned against it, head down, and heaved a deep sigh.

I am acting like a nervous male on the eve of Ashwea Awhidi. I hope I can get to sleep.

He pawed through the stack of storage baskets, looking for something to help him relax.

I know Nadiwani gave me something once; what was it?

He picked up the tiny baskets and squinted at the contents. One smelled like Lavender. Deciding that was it, he took the leaves and sprinkled them on his sleeping mat.

I should have taken a long walk to tire myself out. From now on, I'll have to ask Adia not to tell me ahead of time!

Despite all his efforts, Acaraho could not get to sleep that night.

As Acaraho was trying to get to sleep, Adia was pacing around her quarters, also fussing with everything. *This is the perfect opportunity, with Oh'Dar staying at his workshop with Kweeuu.*

When she finally lay down, she tossed and turned. The morning sun filtering through the light tunnel found her still awake.

A while later, Adia's face lit up when she saw Oh'Dar approach as she sat in the communal eating area. She patted the bench for him to sit and put her arm around him in a hug. He nestled against her, soaking up her soft, motherly warmth. Unwelcome tears threatened to fall, and he sneaked his hand up to pinch them away.

If Oh'Dar had been torn before, his inner struggle was now unbearable. Overhearing Khon'Tor say that he was a threat to everyone had destroyed any peace he could ever find at Kthama. His thoughts were now filled with plans for finding his Waschini family. Even though he was almost a man, the idea of never seeing Adia again, or Nadiwani, or Acaraho, or Nootau, threatened to make his tears fall once more. How could he spend the rest of his life never knowing what had happened to them? His mother and father were still young, but in time everyone aged and grew old. He wondered who Nootau's mate would be, and what offspring they might have. And what of Is'Taqa and Honovi, who were also like family to him?

When I leave, what will they all think happened to me? I must leave some kind of message, something to explain my disappearance. And to explain that they should not try to find me; that this is my choice and that I want them to respect it and let me go.

Nadiwani and Nootau were nowhere to be seen,

most likely not yet having arisen. Acaraho, however, soon joined them. He plopped his food down on the rock surface of the table and stepped over the bench to sit down next to Adia.

"Did you get any sleep?" Adia asked.

"Not a lick," he said, stabbing at his food maliciously, raising his eyes to look at her.

"Me neither." She let out a long, deep breath.

Oblivious to the subtext of their conversation, Oh'Dar had no idea why Acaraho was being so mean to his meal that morning.

"Acaraho? Would you come out with me later and help me gather some bedding grasses?" he asked.

Acaraho placed his hand on Oh'Dar's head and ruffled his hair affectionately. He caught Adia's eye before answering, baring his teeth at her in a fake smile, but his eyes were twinkling. "Sure. I'll be back in a little while to get you. But I must first go and throw some trees around," he answered.

Adia covered her lips with her hand, suppressing a laugh. Oh'Dar did not know what was going on, but he knew that his mother and the male he thought of as his father were kidding each other about something.

Acaraho stood up to leave. "You can bring Kweeuu if you want. The exercise will do him good."

Oh'Dar got up and gave his father a big hug. Though he had grown, Oh'Dar's head still barely reached to Acaraho's chest. Acaraho gently wrapped his arms around the young man, being careful not to hug him too hard in return. At the same time, he shrugged at Adia, wondering what the affection was about.

Acaraho had not been joking. He did indeed go down onto the forest floor, and, finding the largest fallen logs, he heaved them overhead as far as he could. One after the other, he expended his pent-up frustration. After he smashed the tenth one into the stack he had created, he brushed off the pieces of bark and splinters and returned to find Oh'Dar and Kweeuu.

As he entered the Great Chamber, he burst out laughing. Oh'Dar and Kweeuu stood waiting as agreed. Except that Kweeuu was sporting a set of large baskets suspended on each side, supported across the cub's back by a wide, woven band that was somehow secured underneath. Adia and three of the guards were standing off to the side, also chuckling at the sight.

"Are you ready, Oh'Dar?" Acaraho asked. He choked down another laugh but could not stifle a broad smile. *How in the world did the boy even think of such a thing, let alone get the wolf cub to put up with it?*

Oh'Dar was smiling from ear to ear, proud of his latest innovation.

The magnificent Acaraho and his adopted, innovative Waschini son spent the rest of the day gathering the materials that Oh'Dar wanted. Kweeuu was freed from the contraption of baskets so he could romp and play before being pressed into service to carry it all back.

Acaraho watched the lanky grey wolf race through the underbrush. He was a mere blur as he jumped up and down the high rocks, picking up sticks and tossing them into the air as he ran. Acaraho counted back to when he had brought Oh'Dar and Kweeuu back to Kthama and figured the cub still had some months to go before he would be close to maturity. But once he reached his full size, Kweeuu would weigh well over half the boy's weight.

Oh'Dar called for the cub, who immediately romped back. He stood there, chewing on the stick still in his mouth, and bounced up and down a few times until Oh'Dar released him to run some more.

Daylight began to fade, and once Kweeuu was loaded up, they headed home.

It was the evening mealtime when they returned. Oh'Dar intentionally paraded Kweeuu through the eating area so everyone could see how docile the wolf cub was. Oh'Dar worried about what would happen to Kweeuu when his master left Kthama. He doubted that a grey wolf would last long among the Waschini and hoped Nootau would adopt the cub and continue training him. To that end, Oh'Dar made sure the three of them spent as much time together as possible.

Adia spent the day hoisting storage baskets around in the supply room. Selecting the largest baskets, heavy with Goldenseal, Ginseng roots, and Willow Bark, this was her equivalent of Acaraho's tree tossing. She bent over to catch her breath, hands resting on her thighs. Her whole body felt tired, and that was good. After a full meal, she was sure she would sleep well. She chose to eat in her quarters that night, afraid to risk Acaraho's playfulness once again winding her up to sleeplessness.

As twilight approached, Adia prepared for sleep, quieting her mind and thinking about anything but Acaraho. When the room was fully dark, she lay down and stretched out. Breathing in to the count of four, holding it and breathing out for a count of eight. She soon dropped into a peaceful sleep.

She looked around and realized she was once again in Acaraho's quarters. Adia had never been there in real life, but as before, she knew she was there. He lay a few feet in front of her, his great length reaching from the top to the bottom of his sleeping mat.

She admired him as he slept, and while she did so, her heart started pounding. Her breath deepened and slowed, and her desire for him began to swell within her.

She did not wish to startle him, so she willed him to awaken. As if on cue, his eyes opened, and he saw her standing there in the dim light.

This time, Acaraho took control. He rolled off the sleeping mat and stood up. He walked slowly over to her, his eyes never leaving hers. He took her face in both of his hands, bringing her closer so he could kiss her. Just as the first time, it was slow and sweet. Not demanding, just tender expression. He caressed her hair, then slid his hands down to her shoulders and wrapped his arms around her. Her arms went up around his neck, and she leaned herself into him. After a moment, he gently pulled her away, and this time his kiss was more urgent, more forceful, and her longing for him stirred deeper and stronger. He slipped one arm under her knees and swept her up into his arms.

Carrying her over to his sleeping mat, he set her down gently, then lay down alongside her.

Adia looked into Acaraho's eyes and willed time to slow. She did not need to worry. Now that they understood what was happening, he was going to take his time with her.

Acaraho took her hand and raised her fingers to his lips, kissing them slowly and gently, never taking his eyes off hers. She had to close her eyes several times, overcome by the waves of pleasure that coursed through her center. She ran her free hand through his dark hair, then followed it down to where it met the hard muscles of his shoulders.

Being a Healer, Adia had never been schooled by the older females in the art of lovemating, as they did the young females waiting to be paired at the Ashwea Tare. She did not know what to do, only that she wanted to please him as he was pleasing her.

Adia instinctively rolled on her side to face him, laying her leg up over him, drawing him closer to her. Acaraho shifted his weight and moved closer in response. One more shift and he was positioned fully against her. No rushing this time; they lay together caressing and exchanging impassioned kisses, each enjoying the other's desire.

It was so exquisitely pleasurable, suspended in the moment of waiting, that she did not want it to end. But eventually, Adia's need for him won out, and she could stand it no longer. She placed her hands on his hips and tugged him toward her. Understanding, Acaraho finally pressed himself fully forward, burying his desire deep within her. She gasped with pleasure and then again at each slow stroke he delivered. As happened the first time, it was more than either of them could ever have imagined. This time they dragged it out, enjoying each moment, the feel of their bodies finally joined and intertwined, their hands and lips on each other until their movements intensified and they could hold back no longer. And, just as it had been before, after they found release they collapsed in satisfaction and drifted into sleep, this time in each other's arms.

Morning found them as before, each awakening in their own bed. The memory of the previous night was crystal clear. There was no dreamlike quality; it was as real as if it had happened. Neither of them jumped out of bed that morning; they each took some time to savor what they had shared the night before.

Adia made no effort to move, soaking up the delicious satisfaction of the burning longing that had troubled her for years.

As she lay enjoying the sweet scent from the dried flowers and leaves of her sleeping mat, she wondered if there were any differences between what she experienced with Acaraho in the dream state and what it would be like in reality. She would never know, and so put it out of her mind. She rolled over to enjoy a few more minutes of rest. She did not see how it could be any more pleasurable than what they had now.

The next few months passed quietly. More and more, Oh'Dar began staying overnight in his workshop. When not there, he spent time with Nootau and Kweeuu, even making a second sleeping mat for Kweeuu so the cub could sometimes stay overnight with Nootau in Nadiwani's quarters. At first, the Helper crinkled her nose at that idea; Kweeuu was no longer a little round ball of fluff and was well on his way to becoming a full-grown grey wolf of well over a hundred pounds. However, she relented eventually.

Oh'Dar was slowly preparing them for his absence.

As spring approached, Oh'Dar's sadness deepened. He found himself watching Adia and Acaraho more, memorizing their voices, their movements. He did not understand why, but he could see that they were growing closer and closer. It comforted him to know they had each other. And he was grateful for the quiet nights when he could grieve privately in his workshop.

CHAPTER 5

Oh'Dar lay in bed many nights thinking through each aspect of his departure. He did not want anything to be traceable back to the Brothers. As it came time to leave, he would cut his hair shorter, no longer in the style they favored.

Lying on his side, he mentally inventoried his supplies. His new coverings were nothing like those of the Brothers. He had made sure never to use any of their bright dyes. He wrapped his foot coverings differently. The Waschini would most likely suspect that he had been with the Brothers all these years, and he did not want anything to corroborate this. As soon as possible, he would exchange his self-made wrappings for Waschini clothes if he could do so without being caught.

As Acaraho had taught him, he would try to

observe as much as possible before giving anything away about himself.

Oh'Dar had made a small carrying pouch for the locket that he hoped would help to identify his family. It took him many hours to come up with a unique design. He based it on the general style of the Waschini riders whom he had glimpsed as they passed through in the spring. He was finally satisfied that it looked more Waschini than anything else.

He started staying in his workshop longer and longer, getting his family used to not seeing him for a day or so at a time. He would need a head start because he could not travel as fast as the People and anyone tracking him would overtake very quickly.

Oh'Dar fingered a beautiful piece of deep Red Jasper. It was smooth and shiny and hung on a piece of dyed leather. He had made it for his mother, though few of the People wore any decorations.

There was a woven basket in the corner where he had kept the locket and the blanket. There, he had placed the presents he had made for Honovi, Is'Taqa, and their children. He was not sure how to get the gifts there but had made markings identifying for whom each one was. He thought the likenesses were similar enough that whoever found them would work it out.

He would be leaving within days. Oh'Dar buried his face in Kweeuu's soft fur. He could not take the wolf and wished he could explain to him why.

Oh'Dar's heart was breaking. His earlier suffering

over not belonging was nothing compared to the pain now in his soul. It had been hard to feel he did not fit in, but he would give anything not to have overheard Khon'Tor's comments.

Finally, the day came. Oh'Dar put on his new wrappings and moccasins. He collected the locket and the blue blanket with the designs on it. He tucked the locket in the leather bag he had created and then stuffed the blanket safely into a basket he had designed to wear on his back.

In the basket with the gifts, he purposefully left the bear he had cuddled so many nights. Oh'Dar hoped his mother would take comfort from it, just as it had comforted him so many times.

He placed a large sheet of painted birch bark next to the basket that had been holding the locket and blanket, and which now held his gifts. He knew it was the first place Adia would look after discovering he was gone.

Kweeuu was with Nootau and Nadiwani, with whom he had started staying on and off. There was nothing left for Oh'Dar to do but close the door of his workshop behind him and leave. It would be daylight soon. With any luck, it would be the next day or the day after before anyone discovered he was gone.

Oh'Dar was already committed, and though he knew it was forbidden, the only way he could leave unseen was to take the route he had overheard it said that his mother took when she left Kthama in secret many years ago.

He cringed as he entered the female's bathing area, confident that no one would be there at this hour, but uncomfortable at doing something so wrong. He quickly found and followed the exit stream as his mother had done. He could not follow the Mother Stream because it led in the wrong direction.

He stood and looked around, trying to get his bearings because he did not know exactly where the stream came out. Rocky overhangs projected just enough to block any watcher's view, giving him the privacy he needed to get far enough along the path. By the time he emerged where any watchers could see him, they would assume he was just out doing some early morning scavenging.

Having gotten his bearings, Oh'Dar adjusted his direction and set out toward where, last spring, he and Honovi had seen the two Waschini riders cross. He picked his way carefully along the path. A twisted ankle would be the end of his plans. As it was, Oh'Dar was deeply handicapped by his slow travel. Any of the People would have made it to the field hours ago.

He shifted his pack and forged on until he was finally standing in the planting field he and Honovi had begun to prepare last spring. Bittersweet memories came to mind, and he brushed his hair away from his face as if trying to brush the memories away as well.

Squinting against the midday sun, Oh'Dar climbed up the hillside to the path the riders had followed and continued on his way.

It was nightfall by the time he came to the clearing Acaraho had mentioned. Without being able to see the path, Oh'Dar had no chance of crossing the open field in the dark, so he let his back basket slump to the ground. He found a soft patch of moss and prepared for a long night. From his bundle, he took out a sack of pine nuts, dried fruits, and his woven water container. He had experimented many times before he had gotten the weave tight enough to withstand being jostled about without leaking.

A bit later, he lay thinking. *I wonder if they know I have left? Will they understand my messages?*

Oh'Dar knew he had done the best he could to make it clear that he had left of his own accord and that they should let him go.

At the first break of light, Oh'Dar was up and back on his way. He took his time, making sure that he did not vary from the very faint trail left in the open grasses. He let out a huge sigh of relief when he spotted the first tree break in the woods ahead.

The rest of the path was difficult to travel. Brush snapped back in his face, and tree roots tripped him several times. One day turned into the next, and the next. To extend his supplies, he ate violets, dandelions, the blossoming redbud tree flowers, and whatever else edible that he came across.

Oh'Dar had planned well. He had extended the duration of the times he slept in his workshop, so no one noticed his absence immediately. It was only at the morning meal several days later that Nootau mentioned how odd it was that Oh'Dar had not come to take Kweeuu for a romp outside.

Adia had experienced an unsettling feeling for a day or so, but she chalked it up to being overprotective of her relatively frail Waschini son. But when Nootau mentioned it, her heart sank. It had been days. She was immediately angry with herself for being so preoccupied with her desire for Acaraho. She stopped eating and sprang up from the table, Acaraho and the others right behind her. They flew down the corridors to Oh'Dar's workshop. Acaraho shouted his name several times, and then, receiving no answer, flung the wooden door open, shattering part of it.

The interior was empty. Acaraho surveyed the room quickly, taking in every clue. The sleeping mat was undisturbed, and there were no leftover foodstuffs anywhere. It looked as if it had been straightened up and intentionally left in good order.

In the corner was a large piece of birch bark propped up against a storage basket. Acaraho laid it out on top of one of the nearby hide stacks, smoothing out the corners to flatten it as much as possible. There was an unmistakable drawing of Adia, Acaraho, Nadiwani, Nootau, and Kweeuu in front of a large cave. Footsteps led away and down a hill to a figure that could only be Oh'Dar. He had marked it with his thumbprint on the lower corner.

Adia covered her face with her hands, unable to stop the tears. It was clearly a goodbye note. He wanted them to know he had left of his own accord.

But why? She knew he had been struggling again, but for it to come to this? *And where did he go?*

Acaraho handed the paper to Nadiwani and put his arms around Adia. She buried her face in his chest and let herself sob. Why had she not paid more attention to his moods? But she had never thought he would leave.

"Is'Taqa?" She looked up at Acaraho.

"I will go and find out, Adia, but it is not likely. I am sure if he had shown up there, they would have sent word back through one of the watchers."

"We do not know how long he has been gone." She started counting the days on her fingers to when she last remembered seeing him.

"Five days! He could have left five days ago!" Adia turned around and sat down on a pile of hides, tears running down her face.

Nadiwani ran over and kneeled in front of her,

taking Adia's hands in hers. "You know he is alright. You know if something had happened to him, you would have felt it," she said reassuringly.

"Would I? I am not so sure. My eldest offspring has been gone for five days, and I did not even realize it!" Filled with self-recrimination, she could only shake her head.

"He planned this for some time," Acaraho said quietly. He walked over to Adia and placed his hands on her shoulders.

"Do you not remember how he stayed away longer and longer?" he continued. "Sleeping overnight? He wanted to get us used to his absence, so we would not realize he was gone. He wanted a head-start. Nootau, you have been here more than any of us. Look around. See if anything is missing."

Nootau walked around the room slowly, looking at Oh'Dar's tools lined neatly on the stone worktable. He touched the hides that hung from the stretchers. He took his time, wanting to be of some help. Lastly, he went over to inspect Kweeuu's food bowls.

"Kweeuu's food and water bowls are empty. Other than that, I do not see anything out of place," he said.

Adia suddenly remembered the locket and blue blanket she had given Oh'Dar for his safekeeping. She remembered that he kept them in the storage basket in the corner, the same one against which he had propped the birch bark note.

She let go of Nadiwani's hands, grabbed the basket, and opened it. Inside, there were packages neatly wrapped and tied up with green willow branches. On the first was a likeness of Adia. The next had a drawing that was clearly Nadiwani. Then Nootau, Acaraho, and there were even packages for Is'Taqa, Honovi, and their children.

Acaraho is right; he planned this for some time.

She was looking for the blanket and locket that held the likeness of his mother and father. Her heart pounded as she searched through the basket. They were gone, but his toy bear was there. She grabbed it and clutched it to her. Closing her eyes, she breathed in its scent and let out a heavy sigh before dropping back down onto the pile of hides.

"I know where he has gone. He went to find his Waschini family," she said blankly.

Acaraho was at her side in one step.

"How do you know?" He kneeled so they were at eye level and grabbed her hands in his own.

"The locket is gone. The one that you gave to Is'Taqa the night you came and rescued me. The one he returned not long after. It has the likeness of his Waschini parents in it. And the blanket that I found with him—they are both missing."

"I will take some of the guards, and we will set out after him," Acaraho announced.

Adia thought for a moment. "No. Wait. Look at the picture he left. It is clear this is what he wants. He made sure to leave it so we would know he left on purpose, that we would not think he had gotten lost, or was hurt outside somewhere. He wants us to let him go." She stared into nothingness as she spoke.

Acaraho understood what Adia was saying, but he could not accept it. Not wanting to upset her further, he signaled to Nadiwani to prepare something to help Adia relax. He had never seen her in a state like this.

"Come. You go back to your quarters for a while." He handed her over to Nootau, who took his mother's hand and led her back to the Healer's Quarters. Acaraho took one more look around the room before closing what was left of the wooden door, making a note to have it replaced.

While the others were on their way back to the Healer's Quarters, Acaraho found Awan and asked him to post someone outside Oh'Dar's workshop, instructing him that no one was to go into the room until further notice, except himself or Adia. He did not want anything disturbed in case there might be another clue they had not yet noticed.

Nootau led his mother to her sleeping mat, then sat down next to her as Nadiwani placed some cool, damp Catalpa leaves across Adia's forehead.

Nootau took one of her hands in his and held it in his lap. He laid the other gently on the top of her head, soothing her as she had in the past done so many times for him.

"Please do not blame yourself, Mama. I should have noticed too. Kweeuu was pacing the last few days, carrying around the skin toy Oh'Dar made for him. Every time I took him outside, he kept trying to run away. It was all I could do to make him come back inside," said Nootau.

By now, Acaraho had returned. He came over and sat down beside Adia.

"It is no one's fault. Oh'Dar had this planned for some time. But I do not understand why. Maybe Is'Taqa can shed some light on it. I will visit him and Honovi and be back as soon as I can."

Acaraho brought Adia's free hand to his lips, kissed it, and hurriedly left her quarters.

The High Protector was at the Brothers' village before the end of the morning. He had not had time to send word he was coming, so as he entered the village, several of the young warriors jumped up in alarm. The two remaining wolf cubs, also almost fully grown, came over to inspect Acaraho, heads tentatively lowered. He crouched down and petted each of them on the chest, reassuring them that he meant no harm. Satisfied, they turned and wandered away.

One of the young warriors ran off and came back within a few minutes with Is'Taqa following close behind him.

They came to a stop in front of Acaraho, flinging dust and stones in front of them.

"What's wrong?" Is'Taqa gasped to catch his breath.

Acaraho was not expecting to learn anything there, but he wanted to do whatever he could to reassure Adia that they had left no stone unturned.

"Oh'Dar has left Kthama. We were wondering if he came to you."

"Acaraho, no, he did not. I would have sent word if that had been the case," Is'Taqa exclaimed.

"Yes, I know." Acaraho rubbed the back of his neck, trying to relieve the tension in his shoulders.

Is'Taqa turned and told the warrior to find Honovi. The man returned in just a few minutes, Honovi trotting behind him as fast as her buckskin skirts would let her.

"I am so sorry, Acaraho. Adia must be beside herself. How long has he been gone?" Her face was pinched with concern.

"About five days. Did he say anything to either of you about wanting to return to the Waschini?"

Both Is'Taqa and Honovi answered with a resounding no. They knew he had been struggling with not fitting in, but they had never heard him say anything like that.

"We can send a party of braves out on horseback to look for him if you wish."

"Thank you, Is'Taqa. I will let you know. Adia and I both thank you."

As Acaraho was leaving, Honovi called out after him. "Wait! Please! I must go with you. I need to see Adia; she must be beside herself!"

Acaraho waited for her to gather some things, and they both set out for Kthama.

As he pushed the saplings and undergrowth aside, Acaraho tried to remember anything he might have overlooked at Kthama. He was convinced something must have caused Oh'Dar to leave. *Something must have triggered such a drastic measure.*

Not sure why it had not come to him earlier, Acaraho suddenly knew where Oh'Dar had gone.

He must be following the trail of the two Waschini riders from last spring. And I even marked the trail for him with the tree breaks.

Acaraho figured that Oh'Dar was about seven days into his journey—if they were correct about when he must have left. *Accounting for slower travel, he will have crossed the open field by now. He still probably has a good thirty days of hiking before he will come to the Waschini settlement.*

Acaraho knew he had taught the boy well and that Oh'Dar would have taken enough supplies to make a trip twice as far. He could follow the tree breaks, and Acaraho had taught him to keep his bearings using the night sky.

Adia had only told Acaraho not to bring Oh'Dar back. There was nothing stopping someone from following his trail to make sure he was indeed managing.

By now, word had traveled through the community that Oh'Dar had left. Mapiya and Haiwee visited Adia, and the Healer was also grateful that her friend Honovi had returned with Acaraho.

Though certain where Oh'Dar had gone, Acaraho sent both guards and watchers out to search a wide area nonetheless. Reports came back that he was nowhere to be found, easing Acaraho's mind that Oh'Dar was not lying somewhere hurt or trapped while they assumed he was heading for the Waschini settlement.

At the same time, Acaraho sent two of his watchers to follow the trail, making sure the boy did not see them when they reached him. If something had happened, serious enough that Oh'Dar could not be carried back, one of them would stay with him, and the other would return for help.

Adia thought of Urilla Wuti and kicked herself for not thinking to have the Healer make a one-way Connection with Oh'Dar. At least she would then know he was alright. However, she did not have a bad feeling about anything, and no alarms were going off that would indicate he was hurt, or ill, or in trouble. Nadiwani reported feeling the same, as did Mapiya, Haiwee, and Honovi.

Kweeuu, along with the hide toy Oh'Dar had made for him, had taken up residence in the Healer's

Quarters. He stayed at Adia's side and lay next to her sleeping mat at night. She often fell asleep with her hand resting on his head.

Honovi stayed for a few days as company for Adia. Eventually, she had to return to her own family, but Adia was thankful that she had come.

Days turned into weeks. Acaraho figured that within another week or so, Oh'Dar would be close to the Waschini village. The watchers should have caught up with him by now.

Adia was seated at the worktable with Nootau, Kweeuu lying wrapped around her feet. Acaraho made his presence known before entering. He walked over and laid an arm across her shoulders.

"It has been some time now. Do you want me to send someone to bring Oh'Dar back? I am certain I know where he is heading, and there is still time to stop him if you want."

"You think as I do, that he is headed to the Waschini settlement." She said it as a statement of fact, not a question.

"Yes."

"I have gone over it and over it and over it. I do not know why he would leave. Why now? Oh'Dar loved his workshop. He even told me some of his ideas for new designs. You know better than anyone how many hides and furs he has in there to work on. He was not planning on leaving when he had you bring all of those back to Kthama," Adia said, turning to face Acaraho.

"I will do whatever you want. Just tell me," he said softly.

Adia looked up at the ceiling as if the answer was there. She suddenly realized she had been so busy being a worried mother, to the point of forgetting who she was. Instead of worrying, what she needed to do was spend some time with the Great Mother.

She leaned back against Acaraho.

"I need to spend some time in meditation. I will let you know if I come to a decision not to let things continue as they are."

"Will you be at the evening meal?" he asked.

"No, but if Nootau will bring some scraps back for Kweeuu, I know he would appreciate it."

At hearing his name, Kweeuu lifted his head and flopped his tail hard against the stone floor. Nootau decided to take the young wolf outside for a bit. He would bring Kweeuu back after the evening meal, giving his mother some time alone.

After the others had left, Adia crossed the room and sat on her favorite seating stone. It was raised off the ground only enough to let her sit cross-legged very comfortably, her back supported by the cool rock wall behind.

She counted her breaths and quieted her mind. As her thoughts cleared, the familiar window opened, and she was suddenly connected to Urilla Wuti.

In her mind, Adia felt Urilla Wuti ask if they could meet in the Corridor; the world Adia had at first erroneously called the Dream World. Adia answered that she had time, and Urilla Wuti closed the window.

Adia moved from the small seat to her sleeping mat, where she could fully unwind. She stretched out and took several deep breaths. It took her a while longer to relax than she had wished because she was still struggling with her emotions. Finally, the portal opened, not as clear as the Connection window, but there, nonetheless.

The next she knew, she was back in the beautiful clearing where she had spoken with Urilla Wuti the first time. Whiter than white clouds hung in a sparkling blue sky. She had forgotten how intense the colors were. Within moments, Urilla Wuti was walking toward her again—only this time she had someone with her; someone male.

Adia tried not to be impatient. Mundane questions popped into her head. *Why do they have to walk across the opening to me? Why do they not just appear as I do?*

As they approached, Adia stumbled and reached out to a nearby tree to brace herself. The male with Urilla Wuti was her *father!*"

How can this be if we are not dead?

But her heart quickly overtook her head, and she flung herself into his arms.

Apenimon Adoeete caught his daughter up and wrapped his arms around her. She had been a young maiden the last time he was able to hold her. Adia hugged him tightly, her head resting against his chest. Tears of joy streamed down her face.

She finally leaned back and looked into his eyes. It was him; this was her father. All the pain of not being with him when he died came flooding out.

"Oh, Father! Is it you? Is this happening? How is this possible? I have missed you so much. *I am so sorry I was not with you when you died.* I have never forgiven myself."

"Hush, Adia, my daughter. I know it broke your heart that you were not with me when I passed. But you can see that I am still here, and so is all my love for you."

Adia's tears turned into sobs at hearing his voice. It was just as gentle as she remembered. When she had calmed a bit, she turned to Urilla Wuti, her face pleading.

"I know you have a million questions. This is not the time for your head to try to understand, Adia. You need to experience from your heart what is happening now," counseled Urilla Wuti.

Adia nodded and then remembered that they were there for a purpose. She wanted to know what to do about Oh'Dar. But how did her father fit into this?

Urilla Wuti understood. "I could have told you what you are about to hear. But considering your state of mind, I thought you were ready to take another step in your training. That is why your father is here."

Adia's father put his hands on his daughter's shoulders and explained.

"Even as a small offspring, you were extraordinary, Adia. Not just because of your seventh sense, which was apparent very early, but because of your huge heart. You cared for everyone and every-thing. You spent hours trapping the mice that came into Awenasa to release them back outside, lest they were accidentally stepped on or should wander too far and get lost in the tunnels and starve to death. You named every butterfly and bird you came across. I remember when your pet rabbit was lost, and the entire community was engaged in finding her because you were so brokenhearted. Your great heart is your greatest gift, but also your greatest liability."

Adia's eyes never left his. She barely risked blinking for fear he would disappear.

"Your heart is broken right now," he continued. "And that is what is keeping you from realizing that Oh'Dar is alright. I know you believe he is, but weeks passed before you thought of meditating or contacting Urilla Wuti for help. I am telling you this as a warning that you will need to learn to balance your heart with the other gifts of the One-Who-Is-Three, the Great Spirit, as you face future challenges."

His voice was soft, like velvet.

"I know you wondered why you could not stay and be Healer for our people, why you had to leave Awenasa, and live among the People of the High Rocks at Kthama. On the surface, it made no sense, but what I have come to tell you will ease your mind and help you with the difficulties you will face ahead."

Future challenges? Difficulties? She did not ask, suspecting he was not allowed to tell her anything specific. She knew life was never smooth, but it was different knowing that troubles were coming for certain.

"Everything that has happened to you was fore-seen by Sihu Onida, the Healer who was Urilla Wuti's mentor. Sihu Onida had a vision of your future and the role you would play, and she told the High Council that you had to go to the People of the High Rocks to fulfill your destiny."

"*Everything*? You mean that Sihu Onida saw—" She could not bring herself to say the words, not in front of her father.

"If she saw it in the detail you are thinking, she did not tell that to the High Council. It might have changed their actions as your future unfolded, and she would not have risked that. No, she saw your instrumental role in the future of the People and knew that it could only come to pass if you became the Healer of the People of the High Rocks."

"Is Oh'Dar part of whatever is going to happen?"

"Have you already forgotten the dream your mother had, Adia? And the urging that compelled you to make the trip to where you found him? You must focus your training on achieving balance between your heart, your reason, and your will. It is critical that you do so."

Adia dropped her shoulders, took a deep breath, and let out a huge sigh. She had not thought about her mother's dream in years, not since she named Oh'Dar. The dream her mother had the night before she died giving birth to Adia.

"Will I see you again?"

She absorbed every bit of him now, memorizing him, taking in the feel of his arms on her shoulders, the fall of the white hair that framed his face.

"When you die to the realm of Etera, we will be together whenever you want. But if you are asking if you will see me here again, I do not know. It is only your great distress that caused me to come to you today. But I have watched your life, and my love is with you even though you have not been aware of it."

Apenimon Adoeete pulled his daughter close again and hugged her for a long time. She soaked up every moment, wishing she could stay with him forever. She had missed him so much.

"You need to get back, Adia," Urilla Wuti stepped in.

Adia pulled herself away from her father, meeting his eyes and drinking in one more look.

"Remember," he said. "Balance. And by balance, I do not mean to suppress your connection with the Great Heart. You must strengthen your awareness of your other gifts, not dampen the voice of your heart. Remember all three, Adia—the Great Heart, Great Mind, and the Great Will."

Adia nodded and slowly felt herself coming back into her body.

She put her hand to her forehead.

My father is still with me. Somehow, he knows what is going on in my life. And wherever Oh'Dar is, he is also fine. He has some role to play in the future. I know this. I knew it when I first found him.

Fatigue slammed her suddenly. With questions still swirling in her head, Adia succumbed to a deep sleep.

Nadiwani returned with Nootau to find Adia sleeping soundly. They left a plate of food for her on the worktable and tiptoed out. They took Kweeuu and went back to Nadiwani's quarters, which Nootau shared with her, his Auntie Mama. This arrangement had started when Nootau was little because of the danger that he might accidentally hurt the comparatively tiny and frail Oh'Dar.

Acaraho came later to check on Adia and found a changed female. She was sitting at the worktable, having just finished the meal the others had left her.

"I am glad to see you are eating something," Acaraho said.

Adia reached out, took Acaraho's hand, and pressed it to her cheek.

"I do not know what I would do without you," she said softly.

"You will never have to find out." He stepped forward and hugged her to him. Her arms went automatically around his waist, and she rested her head against his warm chest.

It was an infrequent physical exchange in the waking world, and it felt every bit as wonderful as when they held each other during their nighttime visits.

That night, Adia came to Acaraho again. Only this time, they just lay together and held each other, talking long into the night. It was the first time they had been together in the Dream World that they had not lovemated. But it was exactly what they both needed, and it had a sweetness that drew them even closer.

Adia did not explain to Acaraho what had happened with Urilla Wuti and her father, but she told him that she knew Oh'Dar would be alright. He could tell something had happened, and he was greatly relieved. Over the next few days, they returned to their usual routine.

Oh'Dar's supplies were dwindling. He had marked the days on a stone the way Nadiwani had taught him, and he had been walking for nearly forty. His muscles ached. His feet were sore. His wrappings hung on him. He had wisely filled both his water bottles each time he came to a clean supply, but though he still had more than enough dried fruits to last for many more days, he was down to a handful of pine nuts. He was tired but not alarmed. The tree breaks reassured him that he was on the right path. It was only a matter of time before he came to the Waschini settlement about which he had overhead First Guard Awan telling his father.

Then, finally, at the top of a hillcrest, when he was just about ready to give up for the night, he spotted a faint light far down below in the valley.

The reality of what he had done hit him, and his legs began shaking. His stomach twisted. Knowing better than to approach anyone in the dark, Waschini or otherwise, he stepped a safe distance off the path and found a grassy patch to sleep on.

He lay down, staring up at the night sky. The full moon was bright overhead. With his fingers, he traced the star patterns his father had taught him. He remembered many nights of sleeping out under the stars with Acaraho and Nootau, learning about the constellations and how they changed and moved with the seasons.

Now that I am nearly there, everything looks different. I took so much for granted. I focused only on how much I did not fit in, not on all the ways I was loved and accepted. I wish I had not had to leave. Oh'Dar rolled onto his side and drew his knees up. How he wished his mother was holding him as she used to.

Able to travel much faster than any Waschini, Acaraho's watchers had caught up with Oh'Dar days ago. The two had kept as close to Oh'Dar as they safely could, but now they were extra cautious not to give themselves away. They had to be mindful that there were Waschini in the area. So far, the Waschini were not aware of the existence of the Sasquatch. If this changed, it would be disastrous for the People. They did not want a war with the Waschini, but from what they knew, the Waschini would not leave the People to live their lives as they wished.

Morning came too soon, ushered in by the Whippoorwill's call. Oh'Dar awoke to a sinking feeling in his stomach. He gathered up his things and headed down to the valley below.

He sat down to rest about two hundred paces from the settlement. There were many constructions of what looked like wood. Some were lined up on one side, and others were lined up across from them, leaving a big gap in between.

The structures were unnatural, all angles and straight lines. *Nothing in nature has edges like that. How can they think it wise to construct something that looks so vulnerable to high winds and the weather as these do?*

About mid-morning, people started to leave the buildings and move about. He watched them meet in the wide-open path that separated the two rows. Some of them simply went on their way, while some approached others and seemed to greet them.

Well, so far, these do not seem to be the warring hateful monsters I have heard about. But I had still better keep my wits about me.

Oh'Dar decided it was time and stood up. He finished the descent to the valley floor and headed toward what he later would learn was called a town. As he went, he said a prayer to the Great Spirit for protection and wisdom. He had spent a great deal of time preparing for this, but he also realized that anything could happen.

Acaraho's watchers never took their eyes off the boy as he strode toward the Waschini settlement.

CHAPTER 6

Nora Webb and her daughter Grace were standing outside the Mercantile when they saw a young man approaching from the outskirts of town. He was dressed like no one they had ever seen, and he had a basket of some type slung over one shoulder. At first, they thought he might be one of the Locals, but he wasn't dressed like them, and his skin wasn't quite as dark.

"Look, Mama!" Grace pointed at him.

Mrs. Webb took him to be about eighteen. He was tall for his age and had jet black hair. As he came closer, she saw his bright blue eyes. Not one of the Locals; none of them had eyes like that. Despite his confusing dress, this was a White boy.

"Can we help you?" Mrs. Webb asked.

The young man looked at them and said nothing. He reached behind his neck and lifted off a little leather pouch he was wearing. He took out the locket on the chain and handed it to them.

Mrs. Webb opened the locket and showed it to her daughter. Inside were two pictures, one of a man and the other of a woman. Her eyes widened as she looked at the locket in amazement and then back at the boy.

How could it be? After all this time! Is this the Morgan boy? she wondered.

Mrs. Webb closed the locket and handed it back to him. She stepped forward slowly, keeping her eyes soft, and gently put a hand on his shoulder.

"Are you alright?" She kept her voice low. "My name is Mrs. Webb, and this is my daughter, Grace. Who are you?"

"I don't think he understands us, Mama," said Grace.

"Well, he looks harmless enough; let's take him over to Ruby's and get him something to eat. Then we'll go and find the sheriff."

Mrs. Webb reached out her hand, and he took it. She turned and walked slowly, leading him. It was the first time he had heard anyone other than Honovi use Whitespeak, and he had understood Mrs. Webb's words to Grace. He was confident she meant him no harm.

Everything was peculiar. Mrs. Webb led him

from the dirt swath that ran between the two rows of shelters and up a slope onto a wooden path. It felt hard under his feet. There was a roof overhead to shelter the path, also made of wood.

As they walked, he jumped as he suddenly caught sight of someone next to him. He turned to see them looking back at him.

The girl, Grace, said, "He's seen his reflection in the window!"

"Could he never have seen a window before? Where has this young man been? Who has been taking care of him all these years?" exclaimed Mrs. Webb.

Oh'Dar had seen his reflection in the waters around Kthama. But to see a reflection walking upright was a new experience. Mrs. Webb and her daughter were standing next to him, and for the first time, he realized that while he was short compared to the People, he seemed to be tall for a Waschini. He was still young, yet he was taller than Mrs. Webb.

He had let go of Mrs. Webb's hand when he turned to look at his reflection. This time Grace took it and tugged at him to keep going.

They led him into a small place filled with tables and seating places. It smelled good, though different than anything he had ever been around.

They sat down with him and told another female something about *scrambled eggs and biscuits*. Soon a white plate of a beautifully shiny, smooth material appeared in front of him with food on it, and Mrs.

Webb placed shiny tools on each side. He surmised that these had something to do with the food but had no clue what to do with them. So he picked the yellow pieces up with his fingers and did the same with the white fluffy things, eating them both that way.

"Oh, dear." Grace and her mother turned to each other and chuckled.

Oh'Dar knew this wasn't how they ate, but at least they were smiling at him. It was all he could do not to laugh in return. He was relieved that at least these two were friendly!

Oh'Dar continued eating, and Mrs. Webb sent her daughter to find someone called the sheriff. Soon a tall Waschini arrived and came over to the table. He had a peculiar shiny ornament on his chest.

"What is going on, Nora? Who is this, and where did he come from?" asked the sheriff.

"He just showed up, walking along the street. You won't believe this, Ben, but I think he's the Morgan boy. You know, the one whose parents were slaughtered by a rebel band of Locals on their way home so long ago? But how in the world could he have survived on his own?"

The sheriff took a seat at their table. He didn't say anything for a moment; he simply looked at Oh'Dar, who continued eating and tried to look as if he didn't understand what they were saying.

"Well, he's about the right age. But what makes you think he's the Morgan boy?" the sheriff asked.

"He has a locket in a little pouch he wears around his neck. It has pictures of a man and woman in it. I could swear they're the same pictures I saw years ago on the reward posters." explained Mrs. Webb.

"Who has the locket now?" the sheriff asked.

"After he showed it to me, I gave it back to him." Mrs. Webb turned to Oh'Dar and pointed to his chest and then made a little motion as if opening the locket and nodded at him.

Oh'Dar played his part and took a moment pretending to figure out what she was saying. Then, once again, he lifted off the leather pouch, pulled out the locket, and handed it to Mrs. Webb, who opened it and gave it to the sheriff.

The sheriff looked at it and nodded to Mrs. Webb, closing it back up before handing it back to Oh'Dar. Oh'Dar was relieved that they didn't try to keep it, and put it back securely into the pouch around his neck.

"Somewhere in my files, I probably still have that old reward poster. I'll see if I can find it." The sheriff got up, and before he left, patted Oh'Dar reassuringly on the shoulder, holding the young man's gaze kindly for a moment.

Oh'Dar didn't know what a reward poster was, but things were going better than he could have hoped. So far, none of these people were acting like the Waschini monsters he had overheard others whispering about. As the sheriff headed toward the door, Mrs. Webb called after him that she would take the boy back to her house for the time being.

Oh'Dar finished his meal and wiped his mouth on his sleeve. Grace picked up a cloth next to her and wiped her mouth with it. She smiled and nodded. Oh'Dar found a similar cloth on his side of the table and repeated her gesture. She giggled.

"Look, Mama! I taught him how to use a napkin!"

"Come on, Grace," her mother smiled at her. "Let's take him home and try to help him settle down. Maybe there are some of your brother's clothes that will fit him."

Mrs. Webb got up and extended her hand to Oh'Dar. He took it and followed them out of the diner.

It was a little bit of a walk to their home. Oh'Dar looked left and right the whole way, taking in as much as possible.

They left the town area and walked down a little path. Grace skipped ahead and kept turning around, pointing things out to Oh'Dar and naming them as if he could understand.

"That's a tree! And that's a fence post! And that's Mr. Kane's windmill way over there!"

When they arrived at what seemed to be the Webbs' home, Oh'Dar stopped and stared curiously at the many small levels that led to the door. He had only ever seen sloped walkways and rocky inclines. Grace thought he could not work them out, so she demonstrated how to go up each level, and he discovered that they were called stairs. The little girl was so excited to help that Oh'Dar humored her.

Once inside, Oh'Dar started to sweat. His eyes darted from the walls to the ceiling to the walls again. He wasn't used to such a confined space.

Mrs. Webb said something to her daughter about heating some water. Then she mentioned Ned's clothes and going back outside. Grace came over, took him by the hand, and led him through the house and out through a door at the back.

She showed him the flowers she and her mother had planted. Then she showed him her father's garden, naming all the little plants growing in neat little rows.

Oh'Dar didn't recognize any of the names, but he did recognize the plants themselves. Seeing something familiar intrigued and distracted him. He also spotted a set of poles with Washini wrappings hanging on them, obviously set out to dry, and a large stack of firewood beyond the plantings.

After a while, Grace led Oh'Dar back inside to where there was a set of stairs going up to another level. Grace motioned that she wanted him to stay, and she ran up the stairs. In a few minutes, she came back with her arms full and took him to another room that he later learned was a kitchen.

Mrs. Webb was there, setting out a large bowl that she filled with water from a big, black metal pot. Then she disappeared into the back and came out with two pieces of cloth, one larger and one smaller, and a white block of something. Mrs. Webb then imitated washing motions with them. Oh'Dar realized that he was to clean up using the items she had just given him. It seemed that he was to put on the clean wraps afterward, in place of those he was wearing. Mrs. Webb motioned him to go ahead, and she and Grace stepped out of the room.

Oh'Dar dipped the little cloth in the water and was pleasantly surprised to find it was warm. He was grateful for this chance to wash; he was used to being clean, and the warm water made it a very pleasant task. He held the white block up to his nose; it reminded him of the Soapwort root they used at home for cleaning.

When he finished, he bundled up his travel clothes and peeked his head out of the room. They were outside waiting for him.

Mrs. Webb led him to a room at the back and pointed to a raised platform in the corner, indicating he should sit, then stepped back out. The platform was covered in very fine material, much like his blue blanket.

Oh'Dar sat down carefully, and it gave under him. He got up, and it bounced up with him. It was nothing like the solid sleeping mats of the People and the Brothers.

He was feeling overwhelmed. Everything was strange without even a hint of the familiar. It was all straight lines and corners and hard surfaces, and there was little airflow. He didn't know what to do next, or what was going to happen next. If it weren't for Khon'Tor's words, he would never have come, and now, more than anything, he desperately wanted to go back.

Oh'Dar could not help himself. He flopped down on the sleeping platform and buried his face in his arms. He regretted it all. He missed Adia; he missed Acaraho. He missed Kweeuu. He missed everyone. He wanted to go home.

After a little while, there was a knock on the door. The door opened a crack and in looked Grace and Mrs. Webb.

As soon as they opened the door, a little furry figure came running in and jumped onto the bed. It started licking Oh'Dar furiously. He was so caught off guard that he almost spoke! He grabbed the little animal up and dangled it in front of him, its tongue still poking out furiously, trying to lick him. Oh'Dar couldn't help but smile.

Well, what are you? You're all curly and greyish, and you don't look anything like Kweeuu, but I'll bet somehow, you're related.

It was as friendly as Kweeuu and built the same, only much smaller.

Still smiling, he looked over at Mrs. Webb, and she said, "He's our dog. His name is Buster."

Of course, Oh'Dar didn't know what dog meant, but the fact that they had named it meant that it must be a pet just like Kweeuu was. He hugged the little animal to him and felt the tiniest bit better.

"Oh, look, Mama, he likes Buster. Can Buster stay with him? I think that will help!" exclaimed Grace.

"Of course. I'll go and get Buster's dishes, and if he wants, the dog can stay with him."

Oh'Dar petted Buster some more, trying to make it obvious that he did want the little dog to stay.

A little later, while he was sitting on the bed with Buster, Oh'Dar overheard Mrs. Webb talking to someone at the door. It sounded like the sheriff. He heard something about notifying a family and that it would take some time for them to get there. He heard Mrs. Webb say that the boy could stay with them as long as needed.

"I'm sure his family will appreciate that. From what I understand, they're pretty well-to-do. I'm sure when they get here, they will make right with you for his keep. I'm just not sure what you're going to do with him until then since he can't speak and all," said the sheriff.

"We'll figure something out. If it were my son, I would want someone to take care of him, and that's what we're going to do," replied Mrs. Webb.

So I do have a family somewhere. And they're coming here. At least I can stay until they arrive. But then?

The little dog sat next to Oh'Dar, staring up at him, pink tongue hanging out. Oh'Dar lay down, and the little dog curled up against him, behind his knees. Not realizing how tired he was, Oh'Dar fell asleep within seconds.

He awoke to male voices in the house. It wasn't

the sheriff's voice. There were two, an older and a younger voice. Oh'Dar could tell they were discussing him, but no-one seemed to be upset. And something smelled good.

A few minutes later, there was another knock at the door. Mrs. Webb stuck her head through and extended her hand, making it clear she wanted him to come out of the room and follow her.

Oh'Dar got up and followed Mrs. Webb out. She led him into a brightly lit room, larger than any he had been in so far. There was a long table in the center, filled with bowls of what definitely smelled like food. A tall man stood to the side with a young man about Oh'Dar's age. Even though she obviously thought that he couldn't understand her, Mrs. Webb told Oh'Dar that the man's name was Mr. Webb. Oh'Dar was grateful for her courtesy, and because Mr. Webb seemed to live with them, he decided the man must be her mate.

Mrs. Webb took Oh'Dar to the table and pulled out a seat. He sat down as the others pulled out their seats and sat down too.

Suddenly, a commotion broke out as dishes were passed left and right. Mrs. Webb handed him a bowl and with a shiny stick, plopped some of the contents onto the plate in front of him.

Grace picked up a little tool next to her plate and showed him how to use it. It was called a fork. Oh'Dar paid attention because he now knew that they didn't eat with their hands. This seemed a much harder way to eat, but he did his best.

Mr. Webb and Mrs. Webb did most of the talking. She explained to the man and the boy how they had found him and that he didn't seem to understand English. Mrs. Webb had another name, Nora, and he learned that her mate's name was Matthew—at least, that was how they addressed each other. They called the boy his age Ned.

Oh'Dar thought perhaps Mr. Webb and Mrs. Webb were titles, just as his mother was called Adia and also Healer. It was all pretty confusing, and Oh'Dar gave up trying to understand the reasoning —deciding it was similar to their terms of Healer, High Protector, Adoeete, or Adik'Tar.

He understood almost all the conversation, but, most importantly, they were speaking very calmly and kindly. He felt welcome and started to relax a little bit.

By the time everyone else was done, he had only eaten about a third of what he wanted because the fork slowed him up. It was still more than he had eaten in a long time, and he was grateful for it all. He didn't know what any of it was, but it all tasted good.

Oh'Dar didn't know what to do with himself, so he sat where he was while they moved everything off the table. Mrs. Webb and Grace took care of all the food, and Oh'Dar found this division of labor familiar.

As he sat there, he reflected on what had

happened that day. *It startled me when Mrs. Webb spoke; hearing someone other than Honovi use Whitespeak threw me off, and I almost answered! But I hardly know anything yet about what I've gotten myself into. It is still best they don't know I can understand them.*

So far, everyone has been very kind, even the man they called the sheriff, who I think is someone like my father. None of them are like the stories I've overheard about the Waschini.

Oh'Dar knew he would be wise to keep to small moves and take his time before revealing anything about himself. They were so kind that his deception bothered him, but he stuck to his plan.

Mrs. Webb and Grace weren't done clearing away, but Oh'Dar stood up and scooted the chair out behind him. They turned, and he pointed back toward the room where they had left him before. They nodded and smiled and made waving motions as if they were good-naturedly shooing him away.

Oh'Dar was glad to be back in the little room. He was happy to see that the dog was still there. Within minutes, Oh'Dar was fast asleep again; the tiny dog curled up against him as before.

The watchers had followed Oh'Dar as close to the Washini town as they could. They watched the woman and the young girl greet him. They saw him go into a building, come out, and walk away with them around a corner. They could not get any closer without risking discovery. From everything they had seen, they were confident enough that Oh'Dar was not in any danger, and they decided to return and update Acaraho.

Acaraho and Adia were relieved to learn that Oh'Dar had made it safely to the Waschini town and that it was indeed where he had been headed. Nothing the watchers had seen gave any cause for alarm. The fact that two women had greeted him was greatly reassuring to Adia. They had never heard of any Waschini women being cruel or harming anyone.

Acaraho reassured himself that he had done his best by his son. Oh'Dar knew almost as much about how to take care of himself as any of the People. Adia rested on the promises she had received from the other world that he would come out of this safely.

They had not planned on letting their eldest offspring go so soon, and they could not understand why all of a sudden, he had decided to leave.

But it was out of their hands. Whatever was in store for Oh'Dar was up to him to handle now.

Over the next few days, Oh'Dar started helping Mr. Webb as much as he could. Early one morning, he saw the man outside working a patch of soil off toward the back of the house. Oh'Dar had seen the Brothers use similar tools of a rougher design, and planting was something he knew how to do.

Oh'Dar had walked out to Mr. Webb, and, catching his attention, pointed to the tool and made the same motion the man was making. Then he patted his palm against his chest. Mr. Webb understood, handed Oh'Dar his tool, and fetched another for himself.

They worked side by side for the rest of the afternoon, and at the end of the day, they stood next to each other, admiring their work.

The next morning, Oh'Dar helped him plant the ground they had just tilled.

At night he listened to their talk over the evening meal. They never spoke ill of him. Instead, Mr. Webb complimented him on how hard he worked and how much he seemed to know about planting. Oh'Dar was glad to have tasks to pass the day. He knew they were waiting for his family members to arrive.

Then one night at the evening meal, Mrs. Webb said that while she was in town, the sheriff had told her the boy's family should be there within two days. Oh'Dar almost reacted when he heard that but caught himself just in time. That night he had a hard time sleeping, his stomach twisted in knots again.

Finally, it was the day Oh'Dar's family was supposed to arrive. There was a flurry of activity in the house that morning. Mrs. Webb and Grace were especially busy, fussing about. It was a bit like when Adia and Nadiwani straightened everything in the work area before starting a new project. Oh'Dar assumed it had to do with the people who were coming to see him.

Once they were done with the house itself, they turned their attention to him. Mrs. Webb brought him back to the kitchen and the familiar large container of water; then, as she stepped out of the room, she motioned to him to go ahead.

After Oh'Dar had cleaned up and returned to his room, he saw new wrappings laid out on the bed like the first time. He pulled on the new pants and slipped his arms through the sleeves of the new top. He frowned as he tugged on the shoes. They pinched his feet and were inflexible. He saw no improvement over his moccasins, but he put up with them so he would fit in.

I was struggling because I don't fit in with the People. And here I am, with people of my own kind, struggling even harder to fit in.

Oh'Dar tried to banish his thoughts.

Finally, all the commotion settled down, and everyone was seated and waiting in a large room on the other side of the kitchen. They hadn't spent time there before; almost everything happened in the kitchen. Oh'Dar guessed that they saved the room for special occasions like this.

The waiting was worse than the earlier commotion.

Before too long, however, someone knocked at the door. Mrs. Webb rose and went to greet them. Everyone was speaking at once, so Oh'Dar could not easily tell what was being said.

Mrs. Webb brought three people in; a woman somewhat older than her, and a younger man and woman. The older woman's hair was a color Oh'Dar had never seen before—a type of ochre, though darker. The man had the same coloring. Oh'Dar was mesmerized by it.

Mrs. Webb first introduced Mrs. Morgan, her son, Louis, and his wife, Charlotte, to her family and then brought them over to meet Oh'Dar.

Grace gave up her seat so Mrs. Morgan could sit next to him. The lady turned and looked at Oh'Dar's blue eyes and his pitch-black hair, which was straight as could be. She looked at his skin tone, even picking up one of his hands and turning it over. She seemed to stare at him for the longest time, observing each contour of his face.

Finally, she turned to Mrs. Webb and said, "You told me he has the locket with him?"

"Yes. He keeps it in a pouch he wears around his neck. He's protective of it, as you can imagine," answered Mrs. Webb. She turned to Oh'Dar, making the little motion of opening a locket and pointing to Mrs.Morgan sitting next to him. Of course, Oh'Dar already knew what they wanted, but he had to play along.

He took the treasure out of its pouch, and as before, held up the locket, letting it spin on its chain. Mrs. Morgan raised her eyebrows and motioned to ask whether she could hold it.

He handed it to her gently.

Mrs. Morgan opened it up and inhaled and exhaled deeply, nodding as she recognized each of the pictures. One was her son Grayson Morgan Junior, whom they called Morgan, and the other was his young wife, Rachel.

She closed it very carefully and handed it back to the young man, who promptly placed it back into its pouch.

She watched as he stood up and left; the others also watched him go and exchanged confused glances. He returned in a moment with a carrying basket that he sat on the floor. He reached into the bottom of the basket and pulled out the blue baby blanket. When she saw it, Mrs. Morgan's hands flew to her face. She took it gingerly, slowly turning it over to where the stitching was at the bottom.

She traced the monogram on the corner, the initials GSM. Tears sprung into her eyes as she brought the blanket up to her face. Louis and Charlotte looked at each other.

She collected herself after a few minutes and looked up at everyone. She said, "It is him. This is Morgan and Rachel's boy."

Then she turned to look at the boy and said, "You are my grandson, Grayson."

Everyone started looking around at each other, nodding and smiling. Little Grace hopped about the room in glee.

When they quietened down, Mrs. Morgan turned to him again and said, "I don't know where you've been all these years. Maybe you don't even know where you've been. And I have no idea how you survived, but I thank God you did. Whatever happens now, we'll figure it out together." Then she took one of his hands in hers.

Louis rolled his eyes.

"Mother," he said. "He doesn't understand a *word* you're saying."

"I don't care. He can hear the tone of my voice and that I mean him no harm. Think how hard this is for him," she scolded her son, lightly.

Then she looked around at everyone, "I cannot thank you enough for having your sheriff get in touch with us. I'll make sure that you're compensated for your time and effort in taking care of Grayson. I'm not sure what to do next, and we may stay in town for a while. If I decide to do that, would you be willing to let him remain with you a while longer? I would rather come here and get to know him than take him away suddenly. Going away with strangers might upset him," she explained.

Mr. Webb said they were glad to have been of help, and of course, her grandson could stay with them as long as necessary. Then Mr. Webb explained how much help Grayson had been and that the young man preferred to work with him in the fields than sit and do nothing, which, he said, spoke to the young man's good character.

Oh'Dar thought Mrs. Morgan looked very tired. She said she was returning to the hotel and would be back in the morning to spend some time with her grandson if that was alright with Mr. and Mrs. Webb.

As she turned to leave, Oh'Dar got up out of his chair and walked over to her. She turned toward him. Moving slowly, he took each of her hands in his and held them, bending over to look her in the eye and gave her a small smile of gratitude.

She squeezed his hands in acknowledgment and then turned to continue on her way. Everyone smiled at the tender scene—everyone, Oh'Dar noticed, except Louis and Charlotte.

The next morning, a carriage brought Oh'Dar's grandmother back to the Webb home on her own.

After the women had exchanged pleasantries, Mrs. Morgan said she wanted to have her grandson evaluated by a doctor. Mrs. Webb said there was a doctor in town, and they could take him there if she wanted.

Oh'Dar didn't understand what a doctor was. But later that morning, he and Mrs. Webb set out for the walk to town while his grandmother took the carriage she had come in. Grace had chosen to ride with her, thinking it great fun.

When they entered the doctor's quarters, called an office, Oh'Dar's eyes began to sting and water. He wasn't used to the smells and didn't recognize them. Dr. Brooks was there when they arrived, and Mrs. Webb introduced Mrs. Morgan and explained why they were there.

She brought Oh'Dar around to where the doctor could see him. "And this is the young man who wandered into town a while ago," she said.

"Yes, I heard about that. Everyone is saying he might be the Morgan boy whose parents were killed about sixteen or seventeen years ago?"

Mrs. Morgan spoke up, "It was eighteen years ago. I'll never forget it. And he's definitely my grandson, Grayson. But I can't explain it; I don't think anyone can. How could he have survived all this time on his own? He's not a savage, so I don't understand it.

"Would you please examine him to see if he's healthy and sound? He doesn't speak or seem to understand what we're saying, though he isn't an imbecile. Mr. Webb said that he helped around their house with lots of chores." she continued.

"He hasn't said anything?" the doctor asked.

Mrs. Webb volunteered the story of how they found him and took him to the diner, how well behaved he always was, though understandably bewildered.

"Buster loves him!" little Grace volunteered.

"Well, that says a lot!" Dr. Brooks smiled at her, "Never trust anyone a dog doesn't like.

"I'll take him to the other room and examine him while you wait," he added

Dr. Brooks took Oh'Dar gently by the arm and led him into another room. Oh'Dar squinted at the smell.

Then the doctor led him over to a covered table and motioned for him to sit on it, so Oh'Dar jumped up and sat as told. Dr. Brooks chatted away as he did his examination, and Oh'Dar understood most of what he was saying.

The doctor took out each tool, showing it to Oh'Dar before doing anything with it. He even let Oh'Dar handle the tools if he wanted to.

"Now, this isn't going to hurt, but it might be cold," he said as he put the stethoscope against Oh'Dar's chest. It was cold. Then he demonstrated to

Oh'Dar how he wanted him to breathe in and hold it, then back out.

The doctor continued his examination, looking into Oh'Dar's ears and mouth, even having him stand and checking his balance. He shone a strange light into his eyes, examined his hands and feet, and even looked into his mouth.

Partway through the examination, it hit Oh'Dar. *He's a Healer! Like Mama!* After that, he relaxed even more, feeling a sense of connection.

Dr. Brooks snapped his fingers next to Oh'Dar's left ear. Oh'Dar turned his head sharply at the noise. Dr. Brooks did the same to the other ear. Then, he stuck his tongue out at Oh'Dar. Oh'Dar copied him. The doctor broke out into a huge smile and laughed. Then he put his finger on his nose, and Oh'Dar did the same.

This is some kind of game!

Dr. Brooks made a grunting noise. Oh'Dar copied him again.

When he had finished, the doctor gathered the others and brought them into the room where Oh'Dar was still sitting on the high table.

"He's perfectly healthy from what I can tell, Mrs. Morgan. I can't find any reason for him not to speak. He's not deaf, and he's not mute. He's capable of making sounds, so theoretically, he can learn to speak. It is possible he never learned a language. Or it is possible that he has amnesia and has just forgotten *how* to speak."

"Can that happen?" asked Mrs. Morgan.

"Well, it's hard to say what can and cannot happen. This is a very individualized case. Obviously, someone rescued him because there is no way he could have survived as a baby without care. But what happened after that, no one knows. And the truth is, we may never know," Dr. Brooks continued.

Mrs. Morgan spoke. "When we heard that Morgan and his wife were murdered and the baby was nowhere to be found, oh! I thought I would lose my mind. There were search parties out for days. They never found any sign of him. We put up the reward posters, expecting any day to get a ransom note. I waited for years, but none ever came.

"There was no reason for the murders. They had no enemies. Morgan was the kindest man, and his wife, Rachel, was sweet as can be. They were coming back from her parents. Oh, how I didn't want them to leave in the first place. She could have had the baby here, but she insisted. She wanted to be with her mother and trusted her mother's midwife more. It was a senseless loss. Why those savages killed them, we could never figure out. They had nothing of value with them, though we did learn the locket was missing."

No one interrupted Mrs. Morgan. She was reliving one of the most painful periods of her life.

She got up and went to stand in front of Oh'Dar, addressing him though she obviously had no expectation that he understood.

"I wish you could have known your parents. Your father was the light of my life. Your mother was as beautiful as she was kind. You were their greatest joy. I can see both of them in you, though you look so very much like your father; it is as if he's back with me again."

Oh'Dar looked into her eyes as she spoke, his heart going out to her for her suffering. He hated to hear that she thought any of the Brothers could have killed his parents. He knew it could not be true but was helpless to set them straight.

Mrs. Webb spoke next. "You know, they looked everywhere. They found a settlement not too very far from where they were killed. The Chief was very cooperative, letting the sheriff's men go through their entire village. They even seemed sympathetic. We've never had any trouble out of them ever—not before or since. They had nothing to do with the murders of your son and his wife."

Oh'Dar was relieved to hear this.

Mrs. Morgan turned back to Oh'Dar. She placed her hand against his face, and he instinctively covered hers with his. She continued to address him. "Well, you're here now, by the grace of God. And you're healthy. We'll probably never know what you went through or how you survived. So the question is, what do we do now? You'll need a proper education. And someone will have to see if you can learn to speak English."

She turned to look at Dr. Brooks. "Doctor, is he

well enough to travel? I want to return home in a few days, and I'll find a teacher for him. He'll need to learn a great deal in a short time to catch up," she said.

Mrs. Webb and Grace looked at each other, rather woefully. Oh'Dar realized they were going to miss him.

"He's smart, Mrs. Morgan! He can learn. He knows all about planting and fixing things. He helps Papa a lot, just ask him!" Grace couldn't contain herself, and Oh'Dar had to stop himself from smiling.

"Oh, don't worry. I can see Grayson is intelligent. It's just that he needs to learn to read and write."

Oh'Dar wasn't sure what that was, but he was keen to learn whatever he could.

"He'll get the best of care; I've more than enough money to see to that. I want him to have a productive and meaningful life, but I won't live forever, so we have a lot of ground to make up," she explained.

Oh'Dar had no idea what money could be, either, but it seemed to be something useful.

They all returned to the Webbs' house, and as they arrived, little Buster came running out and practically jumped into Oh'Dar's arms. Everyone laughed.

The Webbs invited Mrs. Morgan in for lunch. They asked after Louis and Charlotte. She explained that Charlotte wasn't feeling well after the journey, so Louis had stayed back at the hotel to look after her.

They all went into the kitchen together. Oh'Dar was content to sit at the table and watch, while Buster tugged on his pant legs, trying to get him to play. Oh'Dar closed his eyes and listened. He was comforted by the conversation and laughter between the women while they went about making breakfast.

He felt better about being Waschini. He no longer felt as if he was the product of monsters. He hadn't made up his mind about the Waschini men, but he decided that females were pretty much females everywhere, regardless.

Mothers are mothers, no matter whether of the People, the Brothers, or the Waschini, he thought to himself.

CHAPTER 7

Charlotte Morgan wasn't sick—unless being angry is a type of sickness. While Mrs. Morgan was in town with the Webb family and her newly found grandson, they were back at Ruby's Inn, roiling at the situation.

Louis Morgan stomped around the hotel room. "Well, this is just great. After all this time. *What the hell!* This is just our luck. After all these years, how can this be?

Charlotte Morgan, his wife, sat on the hotel bed arms crossed and lips pursed. Louis could feel her glare almost burning a hole in his back—as if this were *his* fault!

"Well, there's no doubt it's him. He looks just like your brother; the same handsome Morgan good looks. And your grandfather! No one could mistake those blue eyes," she pointed out.

Whereas his brother had inherited the Morgan

dark hair and blue eyes, Louis had taken after his mother's side and had her red hair. It had darkened some with age, but he had always hated it and had been jealous of his darkly handsome brother. At least they had taken to calling his brother Morgan for some reason, instead of the entitled Grayson Morgan *Junior*.

"Well, there isn't anything we can do about it now. The way my mother is fussing over him, you can bet that there goes half the inheritance to *him!*" said Louis.

The days passed one after the other until it was almost time for them to travel back. Mrs. Webb had been trying to prepare Oh'Dar for leaving with his grandmother in a few days, and this touched him. She had done her best to act out what would happen, even showing him with some of Ned's toys. It warmed his heart that she was trying so hard to reassure him it was all going to be fine. He wondered if he would ever see her again.

Oh'Dar packed his travel basket with the clothes and moccasins he had made. He knew he would be traveling a long way away. The odds were, he would never see his family again. He spent many nights with his face buried in Buster's soft fur, grieving for his mother, Acaraho, the only father he had ever known, Nadiwani, and his brother Nootau. And Kweeuu, who couldn't possibly have understood why Oh'Dar had abandoned him.

On the appointed morning, the Webb family said their goodbyes. Oh'Dar hugged Mrs. Webb and Grace. He even hugged Mr. Webb and Ned. Buster danced around his feet, oblivious to what was happening. Oh'Dar grabbed the little dog and cuddled him for a long time. Grace came up again and threw her arms around Oh'Dar's waist to say goodbye.

Soon they were all settled in the carriage. Mrs. Morgan called Mr. Webb over to her and handed him something that she said was reimbursement for their care of her grandson, and instructions about how to contact them if need be. Mrs. Webb gave Mrs. Morgan a basket filled with biscuits and honey as a treat for the trip.

The Webb family waved as the carriage pulled away. Oh'Dar turned so he could keep sight of them as long as possible. Once they were gone, he slid down to hide his sadness.

It was a long and dusty trip, broken up by stays in tiny towns along the way. At night Oh'Dar marked the days on the stone he had started when he left Kthama. He tried to sleep as much as possible, though the jostling of the carriage made it nearly impossible. He kept his one hand securely on the leather pouch under his shirt for fear of losing it in all the jouncing about. He had given up trying to follow the conversation; there were too many words he didn't understand.

It was uncomfortable being in such close quarters with so many people, and especially Louis and his mate, whom Oh'Dar had learned were his uncle and aunt. They both seemed to have very sour personalities.

After what seemed like forever, they finally pulled onto a long driveway lined with trees that led to a sprawling two-story home. Surrounding the house was a wide expanse of green fields and rolling hills. It was very different from the rocky terrain of Kthama, but it was beautiful, nonetheless.

The driver helped Oh'Dar's grandmother step out, and Louis helped Charlotte. Oh'Dar exited last, scanning the area.

The air smelled sweet and fresh, stirred by the slightest breeze. Songbirds greeted him from the trees that seemed to be everywhere.

It was warmer than Oh'Dar was used to, and for that, he was grateful. In the far distance, he could see horses along a fence line. But they weren't the dappled ponies of the Brothers. These were magnificent dark chestnut beasts. One large black stallion raced along the ridge of a small hill, his rich coat gleaming in the sunlight.

Hearing their arrival, several people in matching dress came down the tall front steps and greeted them. They didn't say anything to Oh'Dar, but each did sneak glances in his direction.

After they had greeted those people, Mrs. Morgan brought him over to meet them.

"This is Morgan and Rachel's son, my grandson, Grayson," she said.

They all turned to each other with open mouths and wide eyes and began talking excitedly. As they looked at Oh'Dar and back to each other, they nodded, remarking about his dark hair and startling blue eyes, apparently unmistakably Morgan characteristics.

After some of the excitement died down, everyone helped the Morgans and Oh'Dar into the house, taking the bags from the wagon, including Oh'Dar's basket. He caught up with the man carrying it and gently took it away, patting him on the arm as he did so that the man wouldn't take offense.

It was all he had of home, and he wasn't going to take a chance of being separated from it.

If the Webbs' home was strange to Oh'Dar, this one was even more so. It had an even longer set of stairs than at the Webb's, and a huge entranceway that was used in a similar manner to the Great Entrance of Kthama, on a much smaller scale. But from what he had seen, this was a very large entrance by Waschini standards.

The inside also wasn't plain like the Webbs' home. For a few days, Oh'Dar had to catch his balance. There were patterns on the walls and the floor, and on what he knew was called furniture. And there was furniture everywhere.

So many things in the Waschini world seemed to be unnatural; straight lines and sharp edges, harsh smells and clanking, clanging loud noises everywhere. Traveling in carriages where you felt every bump, instead of on foot or even on horseback as the Brothers did. Even the Waschini clothing was tight and uncomfortable. Whenever possible, Oh'Dar would step out of the shoes they made him wear, much to the annoyance of Mrs. Thomas, the housekeeper.

It was confusing to him that his grandmother had so many names—Mrs. Morgan, Miss Vivian, and Grandmother. His parents had different names as well, but at least he understood when those were to be used.

There seemed to be a lot of people around. Oh'Dar didn't yet know any of their names or what they did, except for Mrs. Thomas.

Mrs. Thomas was the head of all the helpers. Oh'Dar soon learned that she would let him sneak a biscuit or an apple from the kitchen during the day. She was a jolly, older woman with a kind smile.

However, he missed Buster's wet, wiggly kisses and Grace's giddy nature. He wished she was there to help him.

Everything pretty much ran on a schedule. The morning meal was at the same time, as were a midday meal and then the evening meal. In between, Oh'Dar was on his own for the first few days, which he spent wandering around the property.

One day, he saw a man bringing a horse into a large building a way off from the main house. He went over to investigate since he had been around horses from his summers staying with the Brothers. The People didn't ride horses; they were too large and heavy for the animals to carry. But the Brothers did, and were great riders, often holding competitions for speed and mastery. His mother would have been horrified if she had known how Is'Taqa had taught him to ride and how he used to race ponies with the other boys. She thought of horses as too skittish for her relatively fragile son. So he had never got around to mentioning it.

Oh'Dar entered the building carefully, not wanting to startle anyone. The man was putting one of the majestic animals into a compartment of its own. It was the most beautiful mare he had ever seen.

Whatever those are, they're far larger than the Brothers', with unbroken coats. And there are so many of them; far more than there are people. If they don't ride them, what is their purpose?

The man turned to Oh'Dar, "Well, hello there, Master Grayson. I'm Mr. Jenkins. But people call me Jenkins, too. I'm the stable master here. I also direct the work of the other work hands at Shadow Ridge. Oh, I don't suppose you understand a word I'm saying, from what I'm told. No matter, I like to talk, and you look like a good listener, so we'll get along just fine now, won't we?"

Oh'Dar wasn't used to being called Master Grayson. Of course, no one called him Oh'Dar there either. He didn't mind the sound of the name, only that it was foreign to him. He could not quite see himself as a Master Grayson, though it had a nice cadence to it.

When Mr. Jenkins said he directed other men's work, it made him think of his father, Acaraho. Maybe this man was also someone who kept everything running and under control.

Oh'Dar walked past the horses in the other stalls, and they raised their heads and whinnied when he patted them.

"I don't mind if you stick around, but I have work to do," Mr. Jenkins said as he picked up a pitchfork that was leaning against the wall.

Oh'Dar had never seen a pitchfork before. His eyes widened at the length of the tines when he saw it in the man's hands. He exhaled when he saw Mr. Jenkins step into one of the stalls and start cleaning it out. *Ah!*

After watching Mr. Jenkins for a short while, Oh'Dar signaled that he wanted to help, just as he had when Mr. Webb was tilling his garden.

"Oh no, Master Grayson. Miss Vivian would tan my hide if I let you do this. You aren't dressed for it, and besides which, you're her grandson, not some hired hand," he explained.

Oh'Dar signaled again for him to give him the pitchfork, flashing him his most endearing grin.

"I'll tell you what. I'm sure that things can get boring around here, so if you want, I'll ask Miss Vivian if you can help out. *But* she has to agree to it; if she doesn't, I cannot let you. And you'll need some other clothes."

Mr. Jenkins went over to Oh'Dar and placing his hand on the young man's shoulder, led him back to the house. The stable master didn't enter, maybe because of his dirty work boots, but told one of the help he needed to speak to Miss Vivian if she had a moment and could come to the door.

Mrs' Morgan appeared shortly, and Mr. Jenkins explained that her grandson wanted to help him with the horses.

She told Mr. Jenkins that her grandson had helped Mr Webb with the planting and other chores. She agreed with the stable master that he could not just sit around every day while she was trying to find a teacher for him.

"Is it safe, Jenkins?" she then asked.

"Oh yes, ma'am. I'll make sure nothing happens to him. I know what you've been through, believe me. I'll make sure none of the horses are loose when he's around and only let him work in empty stalls. Though he does seem to like them, and they didn't startle at him like they do most strangers."

"Well, he'll need different clothes. I'll have someone take us into town tomorrow and get him some work clothes. He'll probably be much happier in them; he's always fidgeting with his dress clothes," chuckled his grandmother.

Oh'Dar rolled a stone around with his foot while they were talking, not letting on how pleased he was with the direction in which the conversation was going.

Dinner was a huge production. They ate together in another over-decorated room at a very long table. Mrs. Morgan, whom Oh'Dar was to call Grandmother, sat at the end, and her son and daughter-in-law sat on one side of the table while Oh'Dar sat on the other side at her right. There was little of the laughter there had been at the Webbs' table.

Oh'Dar learned what was going on from the dinner conversation. *Grandmother is looking for a teacher for me, like when Honovi taught me Whitespeak.*

His thoughts turned back home. *If it weren't for Honovi, I would be lost now. I must thank her when I see her again*, and he pushed back rising emotion.

His grandmother had plans for him to learn to read, whatever that was. And something called arithmetic. He assumed these were things he would have learned growing up as a Waschini child. She had previously mentioned something about making up for lost time.

Oh'Dar looked over at Louis and Charlotte. *They aren't very friendly, and when they smile at me, their smiles don't go all the way to their eyes,* thought Oh'Dar. He had a distinct impression that they didn't want him there.

He was glad when nighttime came. He enjoyed the solitude. He tried not to think of what Adia and Acaraho and the others would be doing back home.

The next morning, after breakfast, Mrs. Morgan took Oh'Dar's hand and led him outside to where a horse and carriage were waiting. Before they got in, she tugged on his clothes and then pointed to the barn, trying to get him to understand what they were doing. He acted as if he understood.

It's a good thing I could understand what they said earlier. No one could possibly know what Grandmother means from the vague gestures she's making, but she's trying so hard.

The town was much larger than the little Waschini village he had walked into months ago. There were horses and carriages and wagons everywhere, as well as people walking along the sides of the roads. It was overwhelming and very confusing.

They pulled up to a building and went inside.

Before too long, Oh'Dar had two new sets of work clothes and two hats; a big black leather hat and a straw hat for working outside with Mr. Jenkins. Unfortunately, he also had two new pairs of boots— brown for day and black for dress.

His grandmother stood back and looked at him, her hands clasped in front of her.

"You're soon going to be a very handsome man, Grayson, just like your father and his father before him."

She let him keep his work clothes on. When they got back to the house, she held up his dress clothes and pointed to the house. Then she pulled on the clothes he had on and indicated the barn; finally, she made a loop in the air all around the rest of the outdoors. She repeated it, and Oh'Dar nodded at her and smiled, letting her know he understood.

She's trying so hard to help me.

Oh'Dar leaned down and planted a kiss on her cheek, something he had seen Grace do to her mother many times.

Mrs. Morgan raised a hand to her cheek where Oh'Dar had kissed her, and tears came to her eyes. Oh'Dar knew she wasn't sad; he knew that his gesture had touched her heart.

Over the next few days, Oh'Dar helped Mr. Jenkins with whatever he could around the stalls. Mr. Jenkins kept his word and made sure that at no time was Oh'Dar in danger.

A few mornings later, Oh'Dar came in to find Mr. Jenkins tending to one of the mares. She had scraped herself, and the stable master had just finished treating her leg.

Oh'Dar remembered seeing some Yarrow out in the field earlier and went out and gathered some. He brought it back in and showed it to Mr. Jenkins.

"Well, what is that, Grayson? Yarrow? How do you know about that?" he asked. Yarrow was very effective for wound care in a poultice.

"You're certainly a mystery, aren't you, son?"

Later that evening, Mrs. Morgan was sitting outside on the wooden porch swing. It was a beautiful night. Peeper frogs were singing in the distance. Bats swooped lacily across the twilight sky in pursuit of bugs and mosquitos.

Oh'Dar came out and sat down beside his grandmother. She placed her hand on his and seemed glad for his company.

"I was just talking with Mr. Jenkins about you, Grayson. It seems you know something about medicine. He always gives me such good reports about you. How helpful you are, how you learn so fast. And that you're good-natured and easy to get along with.

"I think I'm close to finding you a teacher. I want just the right person, someone who is going to be patient with you and not ruin your desire to learn."

Oh'Dar dug his toes against the porch floor to keep the swing gently moving so she could relax and enjoy it. He loved the creaking sound it made as it moved to and fro.

"I wonder if you would enjoy being a veterinarian. I saw how much that little dog of the Webbs loved you—and how much you loved him. We have to get you into something that interests you. Once you learn to read, write, and speak, you can do anything you want; I know you're smart enough."

Oh'Dar didn't know what a veterinarian was; some kind of Healer perhaps. His grandmother's voice was soothing to him, and he breathed deep, taking in the night air.

"Of course, you won't have to worry too much about making a living. I'll see to that. After your father died, everything was changed, so it would all go to your Uncle Louis. But now that you're here, I'll have to make arrangements for your welfare. It's only fair that you should get your father's share," she continued.

From inside the screen door, Louis was listening. He had been about to walk outside, but when he heard his mother talking, he stopped to eavesdrop.

Louis stepped oh so carefully away from the door. He placed one foot gingerly in front of the other up the long staircase and practically tip-toed back to the bedroom that he and his wife were using.

He closed the door behind him. Charlotte was at her dressing table, brushing out her blonde hair.

"Well, the good news is, she hasn't changed her will yet. The bad news is, she's going to."

Charlotte frowned at his reflection in the mirror before her. She angrily tossed the silver-handled brush down on the vanity.

"What are we going to do about this, Louis!"

"I'll think of something. Mother hasn't changed it yet, so there's still time." Louis sat down and rested his head in his hands.

"He's always in that barn with those stupid horses and that old stable hand," Charlotte said. "But if something happened to him, I don't know if your mother would handle it, Louis," she added suggestively.

"Well, maybe we can kill two birds with one stone. Frankly, I'm tired of waiting around for her to die. If something happens to the kid and it pushes her over the edge, all the better,"

"Don't take too long, Louis. It will look suspicious if anything happens to him after she changes that will. Right now, only a handful of people know he exists. Once her lawyer knows about him, it could cause problems later."

Within the week, Mrs. Morgan finally selected a teacher for her grandson. The teacher would work with Grayson every day in return for her room and board, plus a stipend. She came very highly recommended and was versed in teaching reading, writing, English, and arithmetic to children of all ages.

When the carriage pulled up with the young woman inside, Mrs. Morgan was standing at the top of the long stairs with Grayson.

The driver hopped down to help the teacher out of the carriage. Her brown hair was piled on top of her head, and her long skirts brushed the ground. She had several large bags with her, no doubt containing teaching supplies in addition to her personal belongings. She didn't look much older than her pupil.

Mrs. Morgan waited with her grandson while the teacher walked up to the top to meet them.

"I'm Mrs. Morgan, and I'm pleased to have you here. This is my grandson, Grayson Morgan. He's the one you'll be instructing."

"Good Morning, Ma'am, I am Miss Blain," and she gave a little curtsey.

"Come in and get settled, Miss Blain. You must be tired from your drive. Mrs. Thomas will show you to your room, and your bags will be brought to you shortly. Please make yourself at home. Dinner is served exactly at six pm, and someone will come to bring you down," explained Mrs. Morgan.

Dinner was nothing if not prompt. Oh'Dar had learned to count the chimes of the clocks throughout the house. He didn't understand them all, but he knew the pattern of the one that went off just before it was time for the evening meal, and the one that went off exactly when dinner started and everyone was expected to be seated. He decided that it was somehow like the sounding horn that called the People to assembly.

Miss Blain was seated to the right of Oh'Dar, balancing out the table seatings.

He tried not to stare at her. She reminded him just a bit of Honovi. She had the same gentle air about her, and she had the same beautiful dark brown eyes of the Brothers. She was considerably shorter than him, and her clothes followed the shape of her body closely—which he found appealing for some reason. He had never noticed women's figures before.

Oh'Dar focused on eating without dropping anything, making sure not to react to anything that was said. There was nothing particularly interesting tonight, anyway, other than the presence of Miss Blain.

His grandmother and the teacher talked about schedules and being sure to allow time for her grandson to help Mr. Jenkins in the barn.

"I want my grandson to have every chance to succeed, and I'll spare no expense in helping him. Mr. Jenkins told me that Grayson has some knowledge of medicinal care. Perhaps he might want to be a veterinarian or even a doctor."

Oh'Dar intercepted a strange glance between Louis and Charlotte.

Dinner wrapped up with Mrs. Morgan and Miss Blain making plans to spend the next day going over the lesson plan the teacher had put together.

Later, Oh'Dar overheard his grandmother telling Mrs. Thomas that Miss Blain didn't look even ten years older than him, but that she came well recommended and trained in the latest methods.

Louis had learned to ride as a young boy. He knew how dangerous horses could be, especially stallions. And he knew that Oh'Dar had an interest in the horses, though his mother had forbidden him to be around them when they were loose.

He also knew that Mr. Jenkins left work early on Thursdays and that he and Grayson were often in the horse stables early, since the teacher and the others rose later in the morning.

The next day, as Louis had planned, the two were already working when he showed up. Since schooling started tomorrow, this was the last day Grayson would be with the stable master for a while.

"Well, hello, Mr. Morgan, what brings you here?" asked Mr. Jenkins.

"I thought it was time I started to get to know my

nephew, and since he always seems to be out here, I decided to join you. What are you doing?"

"We're just making some minor repairs to the paddocks. Not only is your nephew a hard worker, but he's also pretty good with tools too. Fast learner."

"I might want to go riding later, Jenkins. You get off early today, right?" Louis asked.

"Yes. But I can saddle up one of the mares before I go if you can take care of her after you're done riding," Mr. Jenkins replied.

"I can do that. How about Dreamer?" Louis suggested.

"Are you sure about that? Dreamer is barely broke. You haven't ridden in some time, Mr. Morgan."

"It'll be fine. I like a challenge. Don't worry; if I do anything stupid, it won't be on your head," he laughed.

The stable master shrugged his shoulders, "Alright. But don't underestimate him, son. Dreamer's a powerful animal, and he isn't that easy to control."

Louis made sure he was back at the stalls before Mr. Jenkins left. He wanted to catch his nephew while the young man was still there.

As promised, Dreamer was saddled up and ready to go. Louis noted that Grayson was sitting outside on one of the fence rails, a safe distance from the huge black stallion. Mr. Jenkins pointed to where he was seated and held up both his palms, telling him to stay there.

Louis was an outstanding rider. Even he had a little trouble getting Dreamer started but eventually took off down the long driveway.

Mr. Jenkins watched him ride off and then turned to Grayson and said, "I'm on my way to the hired hands' quarters, Master Grayson. Best you get back to the house," and he motioned the young man toward the big two-story home.

Both Mr. Jenkins and the boy headed off in different directions, Mr. Jenkins walking up over a little hill that led to the crew quarters.

Louis had ridden down the long driveway but took care to remain in sight of the barn. He turned to watch Mr. Jenkins head in the other direction toward the crew quarters. Once Jenkins had disappeared from view over the little hill, Louis rode as fast as he could back to the house.

Oh'Dar heard the pounding of horse hooves behind him and turned to see Louis and Dreamer practically skidding to a halt a few feet away from him.

"Hello, Grayson. Do you want to try riding?"

Louis said as he dismounted. He looked around to make sure no one else was watching.

Then he motioned to Oh'Dar to go ahead and get up onto the saddle. Oh'Dar had never been on one, and it looked like so many other contraptions the Waschini came up with: overdone and unnecessary. All the riding he had done was either bareback or with a blanket thrown over the pony's back.

He shouldn't, but Oh'Dar had been dying to ride for some time. He didn't trust the man, but he wasn't afraid of the horse, even though Dreamer was far larger than anything he had ridden before.

As Oh'Dar hesitated, Louis encouraged him again by holding the stirrup and signaling for him to step onto it.

Oh'Dar put his foot in the stirrup as Louis had done, and hoisted himself up. As he had done with Louis, Dreamer stirred around when he felt the weight hit the saddle, but Oh'Dar brought the huge horse under control easily enough and walked him in a small circle there in the driveway.

"What the *hell*?" said Louis. He had expected the stallion to balk as it had with him, especially with a stranger mounting.

Mr. Jenkins was getting ready for the weekly card game with the other hands. Those who weren't playing were off in other parts of the bunkhouse resting, playing music, or otherwise entertaining themselves.

They had just dealt the first hand, but in his gut, something was bothering Jenkins. He couldn't shake the bad feeling. He threw his cards down on the table and said, "Sorry, boys, count me out for now. There's something I have to check on."

He came out of the crew house and started walking up over the hill to the barn. He crested the hill just in time to see Louis helping his nephew get up on Dreamer. Mr. Jenkins' feet pounded the ground, dust flying behind him, but he knew there was no way he was going to make it before the young man was up on that stallion.

Louis' mouth hung open as he watched his nephew bring Dreamer back under control. *This isn't going as planned! No matter.*

Angry that the boy had some horsemanship skills, Louis picked up his leather riding crop and smacked Dreamer as hard as he could on the rump, delivering a vicious, stinging blow. *That ought to do it!*

Dreamer took off like a mad demon, Grayson doing his best to hang on. Mr. Jenkins stopped and watched helplessly as the huge beast pelted down the long drive with Mrs. Morgan's grandson a captive along for the ride.

What the hell! thought Jenkins. *My God, he inten-*

tionally spooked that horse! If anything happens to that boy, it will kill Miss Vivian.

Jenkins finally made it to Louis, barely able to catch his breath. While he was gasping for air, Louis started stammering.

"—Jenkins. Oh, thank God you're here! The boy insisted on riding Dreamer. He just took over, and I couldn't stop him from getting on. I tried to talk him out of it, but you know he doesn't understand anything we say!"

The two men watched helplessly as Dreamer continued pounding on down the long driveway with Grayson hanging on for dear life—until both were out of sight.

The minute Dreamer bolted, Oh'Dar had focused on maintaining his balance. He knew he had two choices: look for a soft place and try to roll off the horse, or wait for him to run himself out. The greatest danger was if Dreamer decided to head for obstacles that would require jumping. Oh'Dar decided to hang on and focused on relaxing his muscles so he could match the rhythm of the bolting animal.

To the left was a small hill with a gentle incline. Oh'Dar steered Dreamer in that direction, knowing that this would slow the stallion down. As Dreamer reduced his speed, Oh'Dar tightened the reins in his left hand and with his right, leaned forward and grabbed the reins as close to Dreamer's mouth as he could reach. He leaned back, pulling Dreamer's head down. That forced the horse to slow down, and once he slowed, Oh'Dar was able to get him walking in circles to help calm him down.

As Oh'Dar walked Dreamer around, he patted and scratched Dreamer on his withers, and since no one was around to hear, talked calmly to him.

"Good boy, Dreamer, hey there. Good boy," he spoke quietly and soothingly and made sure he relaxed, so as not to transmit any concern to the horse.

Mr. Jenkins didn't let on that he had seen Louis deliver a stinging blow to Dreamer's rump with his riding crop.

He was grateful that he had listened to his gut. Though it hadn't prevented whatever Louis was up to, at least there had been a witness. And now Jenkins knew that Louis had bad intentions toward the boy.

Jenkins sprinted off to the barn to saddle up another horse to go after Grayson and Dreamer. About the time that he was ready to take off after them, he saw Grayson returning, sitting tall in the saddle and riding Dreamer confidently back to the stables.

Jenkins mounted and rode over to them. Knowing Grayson could not understand him, he still couldn't help himself. He pulled up next to Dreamer and the young man. "My God, Grayson. If anything had happened to you, it would have killed your grandmother. And me, for that matter! After everything she has been through. What the hell was that man thinking? *And where did you learn to ride like that?*"

About that time, Louis came running over to the stable area too.

"Oh, thank God you're alright! Oh goodness. I don't know what happened! Grayson, you had no right to get on the horse like that! What were you thinking? I'm sorry, Jenkins—like I said, he just took over, and I couldn't stop him."

Grayson looked at Mr. Jenkins, and for a split-second, the stable master was sure his eyes were saying that none of what Louis was asserting was true.

"It's alright, Mr. Morgan, Master Grayson is fine. Somehow, he brought that stallion under control. I would never have imagined the boy knew how to ride like that. He continues to prove more and more of a mystery. You go ahead back to the house, Master Grayson, and I'll put the horses back up."

"But it's your afternoon off," Louis gave a deeply apologetic look. He was overcompensating and didn't realize it. But Jenkins did.

"It's alright. It must be done, and I don't expect

you to do it. Miss Vivian will make it up to me another time," said Mr. Jenkins.

"Oh, no. Oh, you can't let my mother know about this! It would worry her so much. No, I think it best we keep this a secret between the two of us."

Yeah, I'll bet you do, thought Jenkins. *I know what you're up to, I'm on to you now.*

Mr. Jenkins had never much taken to Louis even when he was a boy, and now he felt his assessment of the man was accurate.

"If that's what you think is best, Mr. Morgan. You go on now, let us finish up here before it starts to get dark," Jenkins answered.

Louis headed off back to the house. Jenkins looked at Grayson as they sat astride their mounts.

"Come on, let's walk Dreamer around a little bit more to let him cool down."

Jenkins and Oh'Dar rode at a slow pace side-by-side around the area.

"Something tells me that you understand a lot more than you let on, Grayson." Jenkins looked over at Oh'Dar as they rode. He did his best to remember to address the young man as Master Grayson around company. But he used the more familiar first name when they were alone together.

Grayson looked at Mr. Jenkins but didn't acknowledge what he was saying.

"Oh, don't worry, your secret is safe with me. I would do the same if I were you. Best to learn as much as you can about what you're getting into before you show your hand.

"But we have a bigger problem, son. You know as well as I do that you didn't take over Mr. Morgan's ride as he said. I saw him offer the horse to you. And I also saw him whip Dreamer on the rump to spook him. Now the question is, *why* would he do that—unless he meant for you to get hurt. Or worse."

Jenkins stopped his horse so he could turn and look at Grayson directly.

"I don't know what we're going to do about this, but we're going to have to think of something. If your uncle tried it once, he'll try it again. If you look around, it's obvious your grandmother is wealthy. I'm sure your uncle was none too pleased when you showed up. Until you appeared, all your grandmother's wealth was set up to pass to him when she died. Now, no doubt, he has to share it with you. Though I would never have thought he'd go this far.

"Looks like Dreamer is cooled down, let's head back." And Mr. Jenkins turned his horse back to the barn while Grayson followed.

They entered the stables, and both dismounted. Jenkins and Grayson took the saddles and pads off the horses. The stable master gave both horses water, giving Dreamer only a small amount after all his exertion, and then began to groom him.

As he worked on Dreamer, Mr. Jenkins continued to talk.

"Here's the problem, Grayson. If I go to Miss Vivian and tell her what happened, it's his word against mine. I don't care if I lose my job, but that leaves you with no help at all and at his mercy, and I can't allow that. So, since you aren't ready to speak up yet—and yes, I believe you probably can talk, just as I'm sure you're understanding every word I'm saying— then we need another way to expose what he's up to.

"Mark my words, son. Whatever we do is going to be dangerous. But I don't see that we have any other choice. If we don't expose him, then he's going to continue to try to harm you. And next time, he might succeed.

"But I'll think of something, don't worry."

When the horses were groomed and put up, Mr. Jenkins insisted on walking Oh'Dar back up to the house and seeing him safely inside. At the top of the stairs, he laid his arm across Oh'Dar's shoulders.

"Get some rest, son. But sleep with one eye open if you know what I mean. We can't let this go too long before doing something about it."

This time, the boy nodded, finally confirming to Mr. Jenkins that, yes, he did understand. And what everyone had been saying all along.

Noticing the nod, Mr. Jenkins smiled. "Thank you for trusting me. I won't betray your secret, son—or let you down.

Oh'Dar had found a friend.

Louis went directly up to his room after Jenkins took off for the stables. Charlotte came in as he was storming around the room, fuming.

"What's wrong? What happened?" She followed him around the room, trying to talk to him.

"Oh, that damn kid. How the *hell* did he learn to ride like that?"

"*What are you talking about?*" she was blocking him now so he would stop pacing.

"I put the kid up on Dreamer. I didn't think he'd be able to handle that stallion. I thought for sure he would at least fall off and be dragged, if not trampled. But he got that horse under control. Damn!

"And worst of all, that old man, Jenkins, might have seen part of it. I'm not sure. I think he bought my story, but I'm not sure."

"I don't know what you're talking about, so when you calm down, tell me the whole story from the beginning!" Charlotte walked over to a table in the corner and poured her husband a stiff drink. She shoved it into his hand, impatiently.

"Here. Now, tell me everything."

Louis told her the whole story from start to end, including how he had whipped Dreamer with the riding crop when he saw that the boy was able to manage the stallion.

"Louis. That was stupid. Knowing your grandmother's determination, that boy is going to be able to talk someday. And he's going to tell how you convinced him to get on the horse and how you spooked it intentionally. And you don't know what Mr. Jenkins did or didn't see. So now we have two problems!

"It was an irresponsible risk," she continued. "I don't know what you're planning next, but you'd better take a while and think it through. And I hope your next idea is better than your first one!" she said as she filled a second glass of bourbon for herself.

CHAPTER 8

Oh'Dar entered the house and started toward the stairs as Mrs. Thomas came out of the kitchen.

"Good evening, Master Grayson," she said, and then looked at the sweaty, dusty, disheveled young man.

She put her hands on her hips, "Come on, Master Grayson. I think I know what would do you a great deal of good." She led him to his room and made her gesture for *wait here*.

After about half an hour, Mrs. Thomas knocked on Oh'Dar's door. He was lying asleep on the floor because he hadn't wanted to get his bed dirty. She gently woke him up.

"Come with me," she motioned.

Mrs. Thomas led him into a room behind the kitchen that he hadn't been in before. Inside the room was a large tub filled with steaming water. She motioned for him to take his clothes off and get in, showing him a little bell on a table to the side and how to ring it when he was done. She had already laid out a bar of soap and a towel, as well as a fresh nightshirt.

Oh'Dar started to disrobe before she was out of the room. He had only worn his wrappings at Kthama to keep warm, not thinking of them as relevant to modesty.

Oh'Dar felt the water and was pleased to find it heated! He eased himself down into the tub, lay back, and relaxed. It reminded him of the times his mother and Nadiwani would let him play in the Gnoaii— only so much warmer and more relaxing.

Bliss.

As he enjoyed the warm water and the sweet-smelling soap, he thought about what had just happened.

Uncle Louis didn't like me from the start. But why would he want to hurt me? Mr. Jenkins said my grandmother is wealthy. It must have something to do with all these buildings. Mrs. Webb's home wasn't this big, and she didn't have horses, or men working for her.

He tried to put his troubles out of his mind and enjoy what he would later learn was a bath and was also something called a luxury.

As the water cooled a little, he couldn't stop yawning. He stepped out of the tub and rang the little bell for Mrs. Thomas to return.

Mrs. Thomas returned while he was standing

next to the tub. When she came in, she stopped and almost dropped the glass of milk she was carrying.

"Oh my! Master Grayson!" She sat the glass of milk down and hurried over and covered him up with a towel. Then she handed him his clean night-shirt and turned her back while he put it on.

After waiting a few moments, she peeked back around to see if he had covered himself. She then handed him the glass of milk, and with a smile, sent him back up to his room.

Oh'Dar's education began the next morning. Miss Blain had set up a classroom of sorts in one of the many spare rooms. She and Mrs. Morgan had decided on a course of study. Miss Blain knew that Grayson could learn numbers without having to know English, but he couldn't learn to read without it. So, to get a sense of his learning ability, she started with arithmetic.

As with everything else, Oh'Dar was a fast learner. He understood symbols and quickly caught on that each mark she was making on a little board repre-sented the number of apples she had on the table at that time. He was used to measuring when helping his mother and Nadiwani. It was just a question of memorizing the symbols relative to the number of apples.

Wanting her to know he was catching on, he separated the apples into two groups, writing the symbol for each group: 2 on the left and 3 on the right. Then he pushed them back together and wrote a 5.

Miss Blain smiled profusely. Oh'Dar realized he liked making her smile.

Miss Blain then pointed to the group of apples Oh'Dar had just put together and said the names of the symbols.

Oh'Dar felt sorry for her and wanted her to feel she was succeeding, so he repeated the words *two* and *three*.

That made her smile!

"Oh, Mr. Grayson, we're very smart, aren't we?" and she clapped her hands together.

Yes, we are! he thought and smiled back at her.

They continued to work through the rest of the morning, taking a break for lunch before picking up again.

Much later, Miss Blain spoke up suddenly. "Oh, I apologize, Master Grayson. We've gone on too long. I was so excited to see how fast you're learning. I'll go with you to see Mr. Jenkins and apologize. I promise I won't keep you over again," she said, getting up and walking to the door.

She followed him out of the door and gestured that she would go with him to the barn. He was already in the more comfortable work clothes that he chose to wear whenever it was up to him.

When he saw them approach, Mr. Jenkins looked up from what he was working on.

"I'm so sorry, Mr. Jenkins, I kept him over. I won't let it happen again. He's just so smart, and I became so excited at how fast he was catching on!" Miss Blain's eyes lit up as she explained.

Mr. Jenkins wasn't too old to appreciate how pretty Miss Blain was, with her mass of brown hair piled softly on her head, and her lovely brown eyes.

"Oh, I'm sure he didn't mind, Miss Blain," he said, a twinkle in his eye.

After Miss Blain had left, Mr. Jenkins led Oh'Dar into the barn. Making sure she was gone, he explained, "I have a plan, but it's going to be dangerous. And we're going to need help."

The spring weather had given way to the heat of summer. Life continued without Oh'Dar, though there was not a day when Adia and the others did not think of him. They spread the word through the Community that he had chosen of his own free will to return to the Waschini world.

The news saddened nearly everyone, and the

females continued to rally around Adia in support. They all knew how much she loved Oh'Dar, what she had risked to save him, and how she had suffered under Khon'Tor's initial punishment of her actions.

Time was drawing close to the deadline for those who wanted to be paired to make their intentions known. Adia, Acaraho, and Nadiwani sat discussing Nootau.

"I am struggling with it, of course, having lost Oh'Dar," Adia started. "But I am trying to be fair and not think of him as my last little offspring."

"I know. But I am not sure that Nootau thinks he is ready either," Nadiwani replied.

"In the time it takes for the High Council to prepare and announce the pairings, another two years will have passed," offered Acaraho.

He continued, "Nootau has started going through a growth spurt and is starting to change if you look at him. By the time it comes around, he will be a grown male."

"It sounds as if we are struggling with letting him go," said Adia, who had been practicing objectivity since her last experience with her father and Urilla Wuti in the Corridor.

Nadiwani got up and paced around a little. Because of Nootau's superior size, Oh'Dar and Nootau had been separated while they were young. Oh'Dar had stayed with Adia, and Nootau with Nadiwani. Which, in a way, made it harder for Nadiwani.

Adia sighed. Acaraho sighed. Nadiwani sighed.

"Are we saying that he will be ready to be paired by that time?" asked Nadiwani.

"I think that we are all trying *not* to," said Acaraho.

"So maybe we need to talk to Nootau and see what he thinks," suggested Adia.

They all nodded.

"Let us stay after the evening meal and talk with him then," suggested Acaraho.

That evening, the three of them stayed at the table and opened the subject with Nootau. As his father figure, Acaraho started.

"Nootau, do you remember Khon'Tor announcing that anyone ready to be paired should make it known? Your mother and Nadiwani and I want to know what your thoughts are on this. It is a way off yet, but are you interested in taking a mate any time soon? Have you ever thought about it?"

Nootau nodded and then remained silent for a moment. He spoke to Adia first.

"Mama, this is hard for me to say because I don't want to cause you any more pain, and I know how it has hurt you that Oh'Dar left. And I know you miss him every day. I do too. So the idea of me starting my own separate life must be very hard for you."

Adia interrupted because it hurt her to hear his selfless concern.

"Oh, Nootau. Thank you for being so compassionate. Yes, I do miss Oh'Dar, but your father and Nadiwani and I had to accept his decision. And you cannot hold your life back trying to make something up to me that you did not cause in the first place. If you are ready to start your adult life, that is what matters. You will still be with us; we will still be a family. Yes, things will be different, but different is not necessarily bad. It takes time to adjust to changes, that's all."

"It is the nature of life to keep moving forward," added Nadiwani.

Nootau looked over at Acaraho in a father and son moment.

"I have seen how you and Mama care for each other. I see how you like being together. I want that for myself someday. Right now, I am not ready. But by the time the High Council makes its decisions, I might be. How will I know?"

"Let me ask you a question, son. When you lie down at night, before you go to sleep what do you think about?" asked Acaraho.

"I think about you and Mama and Auntie Mama. And Kweeuu."

"And Oh'Dar," he added quietly, eyes down.

"Anything else? For instance, do you think of any of the others in our community?"

Nootau swallowed and smiled bashfully.

"Well, yes. Sometimes I think about Adsila, Etenia, and Cholena. Or Istas. Is that what you mean?" he asked, listing off the names of some of the young females his age or a little older.

Acaraho raised one eyebrow, smiled, tilted his head, and looked at Adia and Nadiwani.

The females chuckled, and Nadiwani replied, "Yes, Nootau. That is exactly what he meant."

"Speaking from our viewpoint, we three think you will be ready by then. And from what you just told us, I now think so even more." Acaraho slapped his hand gently on the young male's shoulder and gave him a good-natured jostling.

Nootau looked down but was grinning from ear to ear.

Nadiwani was looking at him, her eyes stinging. He was the closest she would ever have to family, to a son. She consoled herself with the fact that he would not be leaving the People as Oh'Dar had done. And their family would be growing when he took a mate. And eventually, there would be the celebrations of offspring.

So the family had decided, and Nootau would be put in for consideration of a pairing. Nadiwani and Adia knew they would meanwhile be spending a great deal of time seeking the best possible match for their son through meditation with the Great Mother.

Miss Blain sat across from Oh'Dar with an assortment of nuts and fresh and dried fruits. They were still working on simple addition and subtraction. She pushed three acorns, an apple, a fig, and a pecan toward him across the small table.

He looked up at her and held up six fingers.

She took away an acorn and the fig.

He held up four fingers and shook his head at her slowly, frowning and smiling at the same time. He hadn't been thrown off by the fact that the items were different from one another.

Miss Blain laughed.

"Alright, alright, yes, I tried to trick you. I'm sorry," and she laughed again.

"Let's work on some larger numbers," she said, moving from the single digits to the double digits. He understood the numbers one through nine backward and forward.

Oh'Dar noticed she had started calling him Grayson now instead of Master Grayson. It felt more familiar, and he liked it.

The morning passed quickly as it always did. It was more of a game to Oh'Dar than school. He found he enjoyed learning about numbers as much as he had enjoyed learning about the different plants and flowers when he was younger. Mostly, he just enjoyed sitting across from Miss Blain and looking at her when she wasn't paying attention.

When Miss Blain got up to change lessons, he liked how her clothes showed off her shape and where her waist nipped in and then spread out to become her hips. He wanted to undo her hair bindings and watch it fall down over her shoulders. He found himself thinking about her at night before he went to sleep. He wished his father was there to talk with about why he couldn't get to sleep when his mind was on Miss Blain.

Lessons over, Miss Blain began to straighten up the room. Oh'Dar jumped up to help her, accidentally stepping in front of her. She lost her balance, and Oh'Dar instinctively reached out to catch her. For a moment she was in his arms, looking up at him, her brown hair coming loose from its arrangement.

He was very aware of the smell of her hair, the softness of her cheeks, and her warm brown eyes staring up into his. He looked at her pink lips just inches from his, and it struck him that she was beautiful. A moment passed too quickly before she collected her reason and freed herself from his accidental embrace.

She stepped back, smoothed down her apron, and tried to push her hair back into place. She quickly began picking up her supplies. Oh'Dar started to help her as he had intended to in the first place, but she stopped him.

"No, No, Master Grayson. It's fine; I can do this. Please, go on now. Please," she stammered, avoiding his eyes.

Oh'Dar felt as if he had done something wrong, and it hurt. He waited a moment, but she continued to ignore him, so he did as she wanted and left.

Back to Master Grayson again.

He went out to the barn, head down and shoulders slumped, to find Mr. Jenkins.

Oh'Dar took one look back at the house to see if Miss Blain had come outside, but she hadn't, so he continued to the barn.

"What's up, Master Grayson? Did your morning lesson not go well?"

Oh'Dar shrugged, looking dejected.

"Oh. I see. Does this have anything to do with your pretty young teacher, Miss Blain?"

Oh'Dar smiled sheepishly. *How did Mr. Jenkins know?*

"Don't be embarrassed, son. There isn't a man alive who hasn't had a crush on his teacher, especially one as pretty as Miss Blain," he chuckled, putting his arm around Oh'Dar as they walked to the stables.

Oh'Dar didn't know what a crush was, but he got the gist of what his friend was saying. He wished he could let on that he could speak. He would like to have asked Mr. Jenkins why he couldn't sleep at night, and *what in the world was going on with his body*?

The next morning when it was time for his lesson, Oh'Dar was disappointed to see that Miss Blain had changed her clothing. She was no longer wearing the smooth, tailored clothes that showed off her figure. She was wearing something baggy and loose, like the clothes Mrs. Thomas wore.

Oh'Dar frowned, unable to hide his displeasure. He also noticed that the table they used to sit at had been replaced with a larger one, putting more space between them.

From then on, their lessons were more matter of fact. Miss Blain didn't laugh as much at his cleverness, and he wasn't distracted as much by watching her. And she never called him Grayson; only Master Grayson.

He was learning more but enjoying it less.

That evening, Miss Blain and Miss Vivian had one of their regularly scheduled meetings about Oh'Dar's progress.

"Tell me, Miss Blain. How is my grandson doing?"

"I've had several students, Mrs. Morgan. And Grayson is by far one of the most intelligent I've ever seen. He enjoys learning. He has a quick mind. He's doing far better at numbers than I would have thought, having had no formal schooling. I say formal because your stable master, Mr. Jenkins, said Grayson knows quite a bit about natural medicine, and he had to learn that somewhere. But as far as formal education goes, I can confidently say Grayson has not had any."

"How is he handling his infatuation with you?" Mrs. Morgan asked, smiling.

Miss Blain could not help but let out a little laugh, though she did not mean it with any malice.

"Oh, if you could have seen his face when I came in wearing those baggy clothes. I felt so sorry for him. He looked like a dejected puppy. Truly, it almost broke my heart. He's a sweet young man, and I would hate to hurt him in any way. But it has helped keep his mind on his lessons.

"I hope you know it isn't unusual for a young man to have a crush on his teacher," she added.

"I don't blame you in the least, Miss Blain. I'm well aware of how young boys are. I raised two of my own." Miss Vivian chuckled, then continued.

"It brings up a point, Miss Blain. I wonder if he knows anything about men and women. Perhaps Dr. Miller should talk to him."

"Well, it won't do any good if he can't understand what the doctor's saying," she reminded Mrs. Morgan. "So I guess it's time we move on to English. We can keep working on the numbers, but he needs to learn how to communicate. I can teach him to read at the same time."

"Keep me posted, Miss Blain. And if there is anything else you need, anything at all, please let me know." And Mrs. Morgan concluded their meeting.

Miss Blain went on up to her room and got ready

for bed. The fluffy bed clothes welcomed her like a cloud of comfort. She sighed as she stretched out, enjoying the night air coming in through the open window. She tossed and turned a bit. Every time she closed her eyes, she remembered Grayson Morgan catching her as she stumbled and pulling her up against his chest, his arms around her, and staring up into those striking blue eyes.

He's just a boy! Yes, but he didn't seem like a boy when he had me in his arms! And so went her conversation with herself.

Mr. Jenkins had explained his plan several times to Oh'Dar. He went over how he hoped it would play out, and when he was confident that Oh'Dar understood it clearly, set it into motion. Finally, it was time.

The Summer days were long, and though it wasn't yet twilight, it was past quitting time. Mr. Jenkins and Oh'Dar were still in the stables when Louis showed up.

"You wanted to see me, Mr. Jenkins?" asked Louis, perplexed.

The stable master put down the flat shovel and leaned on the handle. Oh'Dar casually looked over, watching the two men.

"Yes, Mr. Morgan. I need to talk to you about something that has been bothering me a great deal since it happened."

"Oh, and what is that?" asked Louis.

"The afternoon that you asked me to saddle up Dreamer and the horse took off with Master Grayson. I reminded you when you asked for Dreamer that he was barely broken in. Letting Master Grayson ride him was highly irresponsible, I'm sorry to say."

"Yes, you did say that, and I knew it. But I didn't tell the boy to try to ride him. I had dismounted, and he just pushed around me and mounted him. What was I supposed to do? *Knock him to the ground to stop him*?"

"Well, of course not, Mr. Morgan. I could certainly understand that. If that was what happened."

"What do you mean? I don't know what you're talking about."

"Mr. Morgan, I saw the whole thing. I saw you show the boy how to put his foot in the stirrup, and I saw you hand him the reins. And then, when the boy brought the horse under control, I also saw you smack Dreamer on the rump with your riding crop —hard—to make Dreamer bolt."

Now standing straight and no longer resting his hands on the top of the shovel handle, Mr. Jenkins held Louis in a steely glare.

"I'm not going to ask you what you were trying to do, because we both know. And if I were to guess your motivation, I would say it had something to do with Miss Vivian's wealth." Mr. Jenkins kept his eyes pinned on Louis.

"You think you know something, old man, but you had better think twice. If I were you, I would keep my mouth *shut, and if you know what's good for you, you should do the same.*"

"Well, that sounds like a threat, Mr. Louis. And why would I do that? So you can have a second chance at doing in your mother's grandson?"

Louis took a menacing step toward Mr. Jenkins, and Oh'Dar stopped what he was doing and stepped closer.

Louis turned and pointed directly at his nephew. "And you, you little bastard. You can stop right where you are."

With Jenkins distracted, Louis lunged forward and grabbed the shovel from the stable master's hands.

Mr. Jenkins took a couple of steps back.

"You should have kept quiet. It's none of your concern. What's it to you, anyway?" shouted Louis.

At that moment, Mr. Jenkins grabbed his chest and staggered backward. Oh'Dar ran over to him and eased him down onto the ground, loosening his shirt so he could get as much air as possible.

"Get up!" Louis yelled at Oh'Dar. "*Get up!*" he yelled again.

Still crouched down next to Mr. Jenkins, Oh'Dar looked up at his uncle.

Louis stormed over and yanked Oh'Dar to his

feet by his arm, then shoved him away from the older man.

Oh'Dar was watching his uncle's every move. If Louis moved closer to Mr. Jenkins or started to raise his shovel, Oh'Dar would be on him in a second.

Instead, Louis came toward Oh'Dar, the shovel still in his hand.

"And *you!* What the hell are you doing here! You were supposed to die with your precious mother and father. If they had done their job right, you wouldn't be alive. Stupid idiots couldn't follow the simplest instructions. Ha!

"And you don't even understand what I'm saying, do you? Well, listen up anyway, Miracle Boy, while I tell you the first and last bedtime story you'll ever hear.

"It was supposed to look like some damn local savages killed you all. If they suspected otherwise, nothing came of it. Only, the stupid fools got so nervous and jacked up from drinking that they forgot all about you. They killed your mother and father just fine. One of the boys also had a real good time with your mother before she died, if you know what I mean. But they rode off and left you alive. I wasn't too mad at them because the coyotes would have gotten you eventually anyway, at least that's what *should* have happened."

Louis was pacing back and forth in front of Oh'Dar, the shovel still in his hand. "Your grandmother almost lost her mind. We thought the shock would do her in, but no such luck. Because nobody found your body and you and your things were gone, she thought it was a kidnapping, and you were still alive. She kept waiting for a ransom note. I guess that gave her hope and kept her going. And now, all these years later, you show up. You should have stayed wherever the hell you were, just like old Jenkins here should have kept his mouth shut," and he glanced at the old man lying on the hay.

Just then, Mr. Jenkins let out a moan and rolled over.

Louis turned to look at him. Oh'Dar rushed toward his uncle and wrestled the shovel out of his hands, knocked Louis over, then flung the shovel as far down the stable walkway as possible.

Louis rose to his feet quickly, dusting off the dirt and straw.

"You stupid kid. I feel sorry for your grand-mother, her precious grandson coming home all of a sudden after all these years—only to mysteriously disappear and walk out of her life just as he suddenly walked into it. Only this time, I'm making sure you *won't be coming back*."

Louis pulled a pistol out of his pocket. Oh'Dar looked at it but had no idea what it was, though it was obviously dangerous.

"Get ready to join your parents, Grayson Morgan the Third," he sneered, taking a step toward the boy and raising the pistol.

"Are you going to shoot us all?" A chorus of

voices suddenly sounded, and at that moment, seventeen farm hands erupted out of the stall behind Oh'Dar.

Louis stood there, dumbfounded. At that moment, someone else grabbed him from behind, twisting his arm back and taking the pistol from him.

Louis looked around, surrounded by the complement of work-hardened men. About that time, Mr. Jenkins got up from where he was lying and brushed the hay off his clothes.

"Good job, boys. Good job," he said.

The man with the gun motioned toward the house.

"Better get moving, Mr. Morgan. We're all going to go see your mother right now," ordered Mr. Jenkins.

Instead of doing as he was told, Louis bolted toward Oh'Dar.

Oh'Dar timed it just right. Without flinching, just as Louis reached him, he landed a solid blow on his uncle's chin, knocking him out cold. Louis fell to the floor of the stalls, unconscious.

Oh'Dar walked across and stood over him. Looking down at Louis, he said, "I ought to kill you, you *bastard,* for what you did to my parents. But that would be too quick, and far better than you deserve."

The men looked at each other in disbelief. The boy could speak—and very well—though there was a hint of an accent they could not identify. And somewhere along the way, probably listening to them around their evening fire, he had also learned to swear!

Despite the tension, they all broke out laughing. It was the perfect wrap-up and a complete surprise.

Jenkins came over and slapped Oh'Dar on the back. "Nice move, son."

"Nice collapse, Mr. Jenkins," replied Oh'Dar to more laughter. "And you were right; when he thought you were out of the way, he turned his attention to me."

They had known that Jenkins would be no match for the younger Louis, and had found a way to get Louis' focus away from him.

Louis was coming around, and with one hand, tried to stop the blood streaming from his chin. One of the farmhands dragged him to his feet, and they all pulled him up to the house. Mr. Jenkins went in to ask Mrs. Thomas to bring Miss Vivian outside.

Mrs. Thomas came scurrying to the door with Mrs. Morgan in tow. As they stepped outside, Mrs. Morgan gasped at the spectacle in front of her.

Seventeen farmhands, her grandson, Mr. Jenkins, and a bleeding, disheveled Louis were lined up on her front porch steps.

"What is going on?" she exclaimed. She went over to her son Louis, who was the only one bleeding, and realized that one of the largest men had Louis' arms pinned behind his back.

"You may not feel so kindly to him when you

hear what we have to tell you, Miss Vivian," explained Jenkins.

"You best sit down here, Ma'am," he continued, steadying the porch swing.

Then Mr. Jenkins explained the whole story from start to finish, from the beginning when Louis had asked him to saddle up Dreamer, to what had taken place between Louis, Grayson, and Dreamer, to what had just happened in the barn.

"And my men can attest to everything that happened tonight, Miss Vivian. They're loyal to me, but they're loyal to you as well. They wouldn't lie about something like this, knowing the pain it would cause you. We may be hired hands, but most of us have worked for you much of our lives, and to us, you're our family," he finished.

Throughout it all, Louis stood silent.

"And your grandson can attest to what your son did to him with Dreamer," he added, looking over at Oh'Dar.

Understanding that this was his cue, Oh'Dar stepped forward and took a seat next to his grandmother. As he had done before, he took both her hands in his and looked her gently in the eyes.

"It's all true, Grandmother. Everything they've said."

Mrs. Morgan's hand flew to her mouth. *Grayson can speak! And perfect English!*

"Grayson! I don't understand! Have you been able to talk all this time?"

"I'm so sorry. I know that I deceived you. A lie of omission is still a lie. But I hope you can forgive me. I came here as a stranger in a strange land. I didn't know any of you or what to expect. I didn't do it to be cruel," he tried to explain.

"Which of you beat up my son?" she asked, looking at the circle of men.

"I did, Grandmother," Oh'Dar volunteered.

"For what it's worth, Ma'am, it was a heck of a well-landed blow too," one of the men offered up from the back.

As strange and astounding and tragic as the whole situation was, they couldn't help but laugh a little at that.

After the brief moment of levity, the atmosphere turned solemn again. Mrs. Morgan stood to face Louis. The others stood open-mouthed as she drew back her hand and slapped him hard across the face, his head turning at the blow.

"*How could you*? Having your own brother and his wife murdered. And a baby. You took half my family from me. I don't know what to say to you; I thought I knew you, but I don't.

"You aren't the son I raised; I could not have raised such a monster," she said, now sadly.

Louis looked down, avoiding her gaze.

"Do you have a room you can lock him up in? I'm sorry to ask you, Mr. Jenkins, but he needs to be turned over to the authorities in the morning, and we can't take a chance on him running off tonight," she said, never taking her eyes off Louis' as she spoke.

"We can tie him up in the crew quarters with us and take turns to watch him, Miss Vivian," Mr. Jenkins said softly. "I'll send someone into town tomorrow morning for the sheriff," he added.

Mrs. Thomas was standing there the whole time, watching Mrs. Morgan closely.

The farmhands trickled back down the steps taking Louis with them, leaving Oh'Dar, his grandmother, Mr. Jenkins, and Mrs. Thomas still on the porch.

"I'm so sorry, Grandmother. I can't imagine what this is like for you. I don't know what to say," Oh'Dar scooted over and put his arms around his grandmother, pulling her to him and letting her head rest on his chest the way his mother had comforted him in the past.

Mrs. Thomas left and came back after a few minutes with a stiff drink for Mrs. Morgan, who sat back up and looked at her grandson. She almost objected but then took the glass from the housekeeper; if there were ever an occasion for an early afternoon drink, this was it.

"Your father would have been so proud of you, Grayson. I don't know how you survived all these years or where you've been, and I'm not asking you to tell me, although I hope someday you will. But somehow you've turned into a fine young man whom I'm proud to call my grandson. When this is all over, we'll talk about your future and what you want for yourself. But I have to get through this nightmare first."

Mrs. Morgan wasn't going to let herself cry in front of her grandson and Mrs. Thomas. She was afraid that once she started, she wouldn't be able to stop.

"I'm going to let you turn in, Miss Vivian. I'm sure you need to rest," Mr. Jenkins said. As he went down the steps and turned back to wave goodnight, he saw a woman's figure leaning into the window of one of the second-story rooms, looking down at the sight below.

They had all forgotten about Charlotte Morgan.

The next morning, the sheriff and two men came and talked one at a time to everyone involved. They all told the same story, with enough variation that proved it wasn't rehearsed. As the sheriff was handcuffing Louis Morgan, Mr. Jenkins mentioned Charlotte.

"Sheriff, Mr. Morgan has a wife. No one knows the extent of her involvement in all this."

"Where is she? Can someone fetch her, please?" the sheriff asked.

Mrs. Thomas came down a few minutes later with Charlotte Morgan.

The sheriff motioned to his men to take Louis

outside, but not before he saw a knowing look exchanged between the man and his wife.

"Are you Charlotte Morgan, Louis Morgan's wife?" he asked.

"Yes; what is this about?" she asked, tossing her head back a bit and looking him up and down.

The sheriff led Charlotte into the room he had used to talk to each of the men. One of his men stood watch by the door and was there as another witness to each person's statement.

"What can you tell me about your husband's involvement in the murder of his brother Morgan, and Morgan's wife, Rachel?" the sheriff asked as he motioned to her to sit down.

"I don't know what you're talking about. What nonsense is this?" Charlotte asked.

"A little over eighteen years ago, your husband hired some men to kill his brother, his sister-in-law, and their baby son, Grayson Morgan. You don't know anything about this?" he said.

"That's ridiculous. Who is making up this preposterous story?"

"You're saying you had nothing to do with it and don't know anything about it?" he reiterated.

"Of course not," she said, sneering.

The sheriff knew she was lying, but there was nothing he could do about it. He told her she was free to leave and went out to say goodbye to Mrs. Morgan.

Mrs. Morgan was sitting with her grandson in her favorite spot on the front porch. Lessons had been suspended for the next few days.

She had to lower her eyes; she could not bear to watch the sheriff's man take a handcuffed Louis to the wagon. Oh'Dar said nothing, just sat keeping her company, gently rocking the swing.

Having been given the next few days off with pay, Miss Blain came out and announced she was going into town if anyone wanted anything.

Mrs. Morgan looked at her grandson, and he looked at her. Miss Blain still didn't know that he could talk. It was the first time Mrs. Morgan had felt able to smile since the day before. She gave Grayson a wink and nodded.

With a twinkle in his eyes, the young man said, "No, but thank you for the offer, Miss Blain."

The teacher's eyes flew open wide. She looked at Grayson, then at Mrs. Morgan, then back at Grayson again.

"What? *What*?" she asked.

Mrs. Morgan couldn't help but chuckle along with her grandson.

"You mean to tell me that you could talk all this time? Have you understood everything we've been saying?"

"I'm sorry, Miss Blain. I've already apologized to my grandmother, and I must apologize to you as well. It was deception on my part, but I wasn't sure what I was getting into. I knew nothing about your world or what any of you were like. I had no foundation for anything. I wanted to have some advantage while I worked out what I had gotten myself into," he explained.

Miss Blain listened to him. "Well, this changes everything. I'm going to have to redo all your lessons."

Grayson chuckled again.

"I would expect no other reaction, Miss Blain, coming from a teacher," he chided her affectionately.

"A lot has happened in the last day, dear. I'll fill you in later. Go, and please enjoy your days off," said Mrs. Morgan.

Miss Blain shook her head at Oh'Dar in mock disapproval and continued on her way. One of Mr. Jenkin's men stood ready at the curb with a horse and wagon for her trip to town.

CHAPTER 9

The next days passed slowly.

The sheriff pressed charges against Louis Morgan based on the testimony of the nineteen eyewitnesses but was unable to find any way to prosecute his wife. He knew it was a long shot to find the men they had hired. Not only would they not be willing to come forward, but a long time had passed.

Mrs. Morgan had thought long and hard about Charlotte. On the one hand, she had no proof of her daughter-in-law's involvement. On the other hand, she realized upon reflection that they were both not all that happy about Grayson's discovery. Mrs. Morgan remembered catching the tail end of looks exchanged between Louis and Charlotte. She didn't mean to be cruel, but she didn't want Charlotte around; enough time had passed that it couldn't continue any longer. She didn't trust the woman and feared she might even try to harm Grayson out of spite.

Charlotte Morgan had kept mostly to her room over the past days, asking for a tray to be brought to her at mealtimes. A knock on the door startled her. Waiting there to speak with her was Louis' mother.

"Come in; please, come in."

Mrs. Morgan sat down in one of the brocade chairs, smoothing her skirts.

"Good morning, Charlotte. To spare us both, I will get right to the point. Do you have family who would take you in?"

Charlotte hadn't been sure what to expect. She hadn't known if she would be allowed to stay or would be kicked out. Apparently, she was being kicked out.

"I have a sister and her husband back in Boston, yes. Are you telling me to leave?" she asked point-blank, her heart beating wildly.

"I'm not telling you to, Charlotte. But I am asking you to."

"I see. I'm not welcome, though I had no part in what you claim my husband did?"

"It isn't a claim. Nearly twenty men overheard him confess the whole story," Mrs. Morgan stated plainly. "Please make whatever arrangements are necessary. I'll pay for your travel, and I'll establish a monthly stipend for your care, to be administered by a local bookkeeper once I find one. I'll need the name and address of your family to set this up."

Mrs. Morgan got up to leave.

Charlotte stood there for a moment, weighing her options. Her husband was going to be in jail for a long time, that was if they didn't hang him. If she left, she would be out of mind, and Louis' mother *was* making her a very generous offer. It wasn't as good as the inheritance would have been—and living in this spacious home and grounds for the rest of her life—but that option was now off the table. Thanks to her stupid husband.

"Alright, Mrs. Morgan. As soon as I can, I'll let you know when I'll be leaving. May I take my belongings with me?"

"Within reason, of course, though I don't recall you or Louis ever purchasing anything of size. I'm sure everything will fit in one or two trunks. I'll have some brought from town."

The sheriff was still bothered by Charlotte Morgan. He was convinced she was guilty. Even if she only took part in planning the murder, or only had knowledge of it, he could not stand the idea of her getting away scot-free.

He wrote a letter and dispatched it with one of his men to the local penitentiary. He instructed the man to wait for a reply if the Warden thought he could compose an immediate response, but otherwise to return straight away.

Within a few days, the sheriff had a reply. He smiled as he read what the Warden had written. He wrote another letter and sent it directly back to the Warden.

Charlotte Morgan was packing the last of her things into the two large trunks that Mrs. Morgan had provided as promised. In a few days, this would all be behind her. She would be back in a decent city and never have to worry about money again. Not a bad outcome considering she could be sitting in jail like her husband.

A knock on the door interrupted her task. She opened it and stared directly at the sheriff and two men.

They entered the room uninvited. One of the men stepped behind her and pulled her hands behind her back. She felt the cold, hard steel clamp around her wrists.

"Charlotte Morgan, you're under arrest as an accessory in the murder of Grayson Morgan Junior, known as Morgan, and his wife, Rachel Morgan." And with that, the deputy took her out of the room and down the stairs.

Mrs. Morgan, Mrs. Thomas, and all the staff—

everyone—was lined up at the bottom of the stairs, and she was paraded past them. No one said a word, but Mrs. Morgan gave her a steely glare as she was marched by.

The trial was set. Mrs. Morgan insisted on attending. She knew it would be painful but needed to have clear in her mind just what her son and daughter-in-law had done so she could deal with it and move forward. With many years still to live, she hoped, she wanted to be there for her grandson. He was all she had left.

Because they had his confession, the trial of Louis Morgan was cut and dried. There were enough witnesses that Grayson didn't need to be called. Mrs. Morgan wanted to spare him the scrutiny—she wasn't sure if they could raise questions about his past but didn't want to risk the possibility out of respect for his privacy.

The trial of Charlotte Morgan was more involved. The sheriff's note had indeed uncovered information concerning her involvement. Whether the jury would believe her or two convicted inmates was yet to be seen.

There is something about human nature that drives men to confess their crimes to *someone* at some point—even another inmate—in some cases perhaps bragging; in others a need to purge their consciences.

No matter what their motivation, the sheriff's note to the Warden had produced two men who claimed they were hired by Louis and Charlotte Morgan to kill Morgan and Rachel Morgan, and their baby. Both the men were willing to talk in return for a reduced sentence. Considering the heinous nature of their crime, everyone involved was willing to make the deal.

Mrs. Morgan listened intently to the first man's testimony, steeling herself for what she was about to hear.

After he was sworn in, the prosecutor asked the man to tell the court what had happened.

"It was about eighteen years ago, thereabouts. This fancy dressed man who said his name was Louis Morgan hired us to track down his brother and the brother's wife on their way back home. We found them easily enough because there was only one route back from where they were coming. We scouted out a place to kill them, and then as they drove near, we came up behind them. The man had a rifle, so it took both of us to handle him. Once he was out of the way, the woman was easy. Before we killed her, my partner decided to have a little fun with her, if you know what I mean."

The prosecutor said no that they didn't know what he meant and that he needed to explain.

Having no fear of prosecution, the man went on to tell the jury that his partner had raped the woman before killing her. Then he recounted how they had scalped both, trying to make it look like a raid by a band of Locals.

"Was there any more to the plan that you haven't told us?" the prosecutor asked.

"Well, there was supposed to be a baby somewhere, but by then, we were pretty nervous, and the excitement was wearing off. My partner thought he saw something big, very big, moving through the treeline way up on the ridge, so we hurried up and left. We figured later that whatever it was probably took care of the brat—either that or the coyotes would get it," he finished up.

"In your meeting with Louis Morgan, was his wife ever in the room when this was discussed?"

"Yeah, she was there the whole time. Even made suggestions about how to do it," said the man.

Then, to sweeten the pot, though no one could know if this was true, he added,

"To me, she even looked like she enjoyed the idea of it all," he smiled, staring at Charlotte, who was sitting at one of the tables and glared daggers back at him.

The next inmate was called and gave similar testimony. He left out the part about raping Rachel Morgan, but did say that Charlotte Morgan was involved in it too—not just the planning, but was also there when Louis Morgan called them out on not killing the baby.

Mrs. Morgan sat stoically through it all. In the end, both Louis and his wife were found guilty of planning the murders of Rachel Morgan and Grayson Morgan. Had Mrs. Morgan and her deceased husband not been people of influence, Louis and Charlotte would have received far worse treatment for their crimes. Punishments were brutal and severe. Many would have argued that they deserved to suffer for what they did, but Mrs. Morgan had to live with herself, so she made arrangements for permanent incarceration but no hard labor. It was far better than they deserved.

It took a while for life to return to normal, but as hard as it was, the trial and sentencing were the closure that Mrs. Morgan needed to help her start the healing process. That, and changing her will to leave everything to Grayson Stone Morgan the Third.

Miss Blain met with Mrs. Morgan to map out a new course of study.

"Now that we know Master Grayson can understand and speak English, I'll focus on reading—unless he already knows how to do that, too!"

"That boy is one surprise after another, it's true," and Mrs. Morgan chuckled.

Grayson didn't know how to read, so they turned their focus to that. He seemed fascinated with learning the different letters and how to form them. They couldn't know that, to him, it was like the tunnel markings at Kthama, only on a far more complex scale.

A whole new world was opening up for young Master Grayson.

Summer turned to fall, and fall gave way to winter. Oh'Dar was reading at an exceptional level, and his writing skills were equally developed.

Miss Blain met again with Mrs. Morgan.

"Your grandson is mastering everything I throw at him. We need to talk about his future and what you envision for him. And of course, what he wants for himself."

"Do you have any ideas, Miss Blain? You're working with him every day."

"It's hard to narrow down because, truthfully, he's smart enough to do anything he wants. At first, I thought perhaps bookkeeping as he's so good with numbers. But he seems to have a passion for herbs and healing, as we've discussed before. He's also very good with the horses. I think he could easily become a veterinarian, or even a doctor if he were inclined."

Mrs. Morgan fell silent for a moment. That would mean sending Grayson off for medical instruction at a hospital in a large city. He would only be home on holidays and long breaks. It made her sad to think of not seeing him every day.

"Why don't we call him in now and see what he wants to do?" Mrs. Morgan suggested.

She rang a bell, and Mrs. Thomas appeared. In a few minutes, she returned with Grayson.

Though it had only been a few months, her grandson had changed. Working with Mr. Jenkins, he had developed a more muscular build. His jet-black hair offset his startling blue eyes, and he was turning into a handsome young man. Mrs. Morgan could only imagine the attention he would get at school, especially coming from a wealthy family. She secretly hoped that he would pick medical training as there would be few young women there.

Does he know anything about girls? she wondered. He had a crush on Miss Blain, so she knew he was interested in them by now.

Mrs. Morgan patted the seat beside her on the chaise.

"Grayson, Miss Blain tells me that you're making great progress in your lessons. She says that you have an appetite for learning and have exceeded her expectations in all your studies."

Oh'Dar smiled on hearing that Miss Blain had praised him. He gave her a sideways glance, and she returned it before lowering her eyes.

His grandmother spoke again. "Soon, you'll need a higher level of instruction. We want to know what you're interested in. Have you thought about what you might want to do with the rest of your life?" she asked.

Oh'Dar thought of several replies, none of which would be appropriate considering that Miss Blain was trying to act as if she wasn't interested in him.

"Are you asking me what I want to become? Like a lawyer or a stable master?" he clarified, using some of the few work titles he knew.

"Yes. What would you like to do?"

Oh'Dar had already spent some time thinking about that. He knew he was growing up, and regardless of his grandmother's wealth, wanted to be able to provide for a family if he ever had one. He remembered Dr. Brooks and his realization that the doctor was a Healer like his mother.

"I would like to become a doctor," he answered. "If you think I'm smart enough." He had overheard enough conversation to know that it took a great deal of learning to become a doctor.

"I *know* you're smart enough, Grayson. You can do anything you put your mind to, I do not doubt," Miss Blain replied.

"Well then, we'll work to that end," said Mrs. Morgan. "It will mean that you have to go off on your own to a much larger town than any you've seen so far. But we'll do our best to prepare you, so it isn't so overwhelming. You've been through harder things than that, I'm certain," she reassured him.

Oh'Dar frowned and pressed his lips together.

"But you'll be able to come home on long breaks and at other times. It isn't like we won't see each other."

His grandmother patted his hand. "Oh, don't worry, Grayson. It is still a way off, and we'll do everything we can to make it as easy on you as possible. Who knows, maybe I'll even come out and visit you there!" she added.

"Oh, that would be wonderful. I can't bear the idea of being away from you very long, Grandmother," he said.

"Well, then it's settled. But, as I said, it is still a way off, so let's enjoy our time together now and make the most of it. Please don't worry; I'm not as old as you think I am, and I'm not going anywhere," she added.

Oh'Dar and Miss Blain spent the rest of the winter continuing to work on his skills. After the lessons, he still helped Mr. Jenkins in the barn with the horses. He had even taken to riding Dreamer, now that his grandmother was assured he wouldn't get hurt.

Miss Blain stood at the fence watching Grayson Stone Morgan the Third riding the big black stallion around the property. He was a riveting sight, looking even taller mounted on the horse, his black hair and black riding boots matching the steed. His command of the powerful animal made her heart race. She could not keep her eyes off him. She could only imagine how he would become even more handsome as the rest of his build developed.

I have to get this under control. Grayson's schoolboy crush on me is one thing, but I'm starting to think about him inappropriately. I'm a grown woman. It's my responsibility to hold the line. Oh, but he doesn't look like a boy!

Stop it. Stop it! You're easily ten years older than him. He's going off to school. And you cannot betray Mrs. Morgan's trust, she scolded herself.

She turned and walked away. *If I don't get myself under control, Mrs. Morgan is going to have to find another teacher for her grandson.*

Time passed, and Miss Blain continued to work with her pupil on reading and writing, making sure to keep things on a professional level. Miss Blain was keeping herself under control, but she couldn't know that Master Grayson was struggling more and more.

Miss Blain was working diligently to prepare him for the next step in his education, so he had a lot of ground to make up. Though he was reading and writing, he lacked other subjects. She wondered if it were time for another teacher. Perhaps she had taken

Grayson as far as she could. She didn't want to hold him back.

One evening, Miss Blain broached the subject with Mrs. Morgan.

"Mrs. Morgan, in my opinion, Master Grayson has fully grasped reading and writing. His arithmetic skills are excellent, but he needs to study advanced arithmetic, history, and other subjects. I've taken him as far as I can."

Mrs. Morgan set down her tea and sighed.

"I'm sorry to hear that, but I appreciate your honesty. I'm pleased my grandson is doing so well. You've done an excellent job with him, Miss Blain. And I know there have been challenges," and she gave the teacher a knowing smile. "Do you have anyone you would recommend?"

"Well, I know of several teachers whom I think would be very good." She paused a moment before continuing, "May I please speak openly, Mrs. Morgan?"

"Please do, my dear."

"Your grandson is a very fine-looking young man. And he's going to become more handsome as he matures. Considering that, and his lack of experience, so to speak, coupled with the fact that he's in a position to inherit a great deal of wealth; oh dear—" She stopped, embarrassed.

"No, please. Please go on. I think I know where you're going with this. There's nothing to be embarrassed about; we're both women."

"Not everyone is scrupulous. It would be easy for someone to take advantage of his innocence. I know he must travel away from home to get the advanced instruction he needs. I would hate to see those plans derailed by someone looking to land herself a wealthy, good looking husband." She sighed, finally having said it.

"I'm grateful to you, Miss Blain, for holding the line with my grandson. I see the way he still looks at you. If anything, it has gotten worse. Had you been a lesser person, it all could have gone in an awful direction for Grayson."

Mrs. Morgan got up and walked over to the mantel. Then she turned around and continued.

"Perhaps the best thing for my grandson's continued education is that when you give me your list of recommendations, you should make sure there are only *male* teachers on the list."

"Yes, I'll do that," she laughed, relieved that she hadn't offended Mrs. Morgan and that no one would be taking advantage of Grayson—at least not while he was under his grandmother's roof.

The next morning, Miss Blain worked on her list. By the end of the day, she had handed it to Mrs. Morgan, who got to work investigating each teacher's credentials and character.

The day came when Mrs. Morgan had located a new teacher for Oh'Dar. He would arrive in several days, and it was time to tell her grandson, though she dreaded it. She knew that Miss Blain's departure would break his heart.

That afternoon, Mrs. Morgan called Oh'Dar in to talk with her and Miss Blain. He entered the over-furnished room and sat down next to his grandmother, though he wanted to sit down next to Miss Blain.

The teacher spoke first. "Master Grayson. First of all, I must say that I've never had a student as bright and as willing to learn as you've been. I'm confident that if you only needed basic arithmetic, reading, and writing skills you would be ready now. But unfortunately, to become a doctor, there is more you have to learn, and I am not able to teach you those things."

Oh'Dar didn't like where this was going. When his grandmother spoke up, it got even worse.

"Miss Blain has been candid with me in saying that she has taken you as far as she can and that now it is time for you to have a different teacher. This wasn't an easy thing for her to tell me, Grayson. She thinks very highly of you and hates to lose you as a student," his grandmother tried to explain.

Student? That's how she thinks of me, as her student? Is that all?

Oh'Dar was struggling to control his disappointment. It was more than disappointment, though; he was heartbroken.

"So, are you leaving?" his voice broke a little bit, embarrassing him.

"Yes, I'm sorry to say. Your new teacher will arrive in four or five days."

"I see. I would like to be excused now, please, Grandmother." Oh'Dar got up without being dismissed and didn't wait for her permission to leave the room.

He walked up the stairs to his room as fast as he could without running. He closed the door and turned off the light. He laid down on the soft sweet-smelling comforter and curled on his side the way he had as a youngster when he needed comforting.

I'm never going to see her again. I've come all this way, and I'm still alone. When am I ever going to be happy? Maybe I should have stayed at Kthama.

Master Grayson didn't come down for dinner. His grandmother sent up a tray, but it came back untouched.

Mrs. Morgan felt terrible for him. This was his first crush and his first heartache. How she wished his father was there to help him through it. Doing something she seldom did, she decided to walk out to the barn to ask for Mr. Jenkins' help.

Mr. Jenkins was more than surprised to see Miss Vivian walking toward him. He ran over to meet her, fearing something was wrong.

He swept his hat off his head and said, "Ma'am?!"

"Everything's fine, Mr. Jenkins, I just wanted to talk to you privately, that's all."

"Here, sit over here."

"No, I can stand; it's not going to take very long. Mr. Jenkins, Miss Blain will be leaving soon. She says that she cannot teach Grayson anything further and that he needs another teacher to keep moving forward if he wants to become a doctor. As you can imagine, he's heartbroken. His father isn't here, and I don't know what to say to him. Do you think you could try to help him?"

"I'll be glad to try, Miss Vivian. I guess we've all seen the way he looks at Miss Blain."

"Thank you, Mr. Jenkins. As always, I knew I could count on you. We're going to miss him when he goes away, aren't we, old friend," she said as a statement, not a question.

It was the first time she had alluded to the fact that they had a long history together and were more like family than employer and employee.

"Yes, Miss Vivian, we are. That's a fact."

The next day Oh'Dar finally came out of his room. He had no heart for his lessons. Miss Blain could see that he was miserable, so she cut the day short.

Before he left her, he said, head down, without turning to face her, "Just please promise me you won't leave without saying goodbye."

"I promise, Master Grayson," she answered quietly.

Oh'Dar went directly to the barn. He wanted to get away from the house, and he had spent too much time cooped up in his room. He knew that some hard work would help him process his feelings.

He picked up a flat shovel and began mucking out one of the stalls. Mr. Jenkins heard the scraping of the metal against the floor and found him.

"Hello, son, I heard Miss Blain is leaving. I guess that's the reason you're trying to scrape a layer of metal off that shovel?"

Oh'Dar stopped shoveling.

"What am I going to do?" he asked.

"There isn't much you can do, son. I know it hurts. I remember the first time I got my heart broken. I thought I was going to die, it hurt so bad. I know it doesn't help much to tell you this now, but it will pass. You're young. You don't think so, but over time you'll meet lots of young ladies your age. Miss Blain is a little bit older than you, you know."

"I don't care about that. Besides, she isn't that much older. Age doesn't matter. Why, look at you and Grandmother!"

"What?" Mr. Jenkins stopped cold.

"What are you talking about—your grandmother and me?"

"I've seen you two together. Are you saying you don't know that you like each other?" Oh'Dar was shocked. It was so obvious to him.

"Well I don't know what you're talking about, truly I don't. I just know that you will get over Miss Blain. You don't believe me, but you'll forget her."

"I don't want to forget her. And I don't want her to forget *me,*" he said.

Jenkins felt bad for the young man. He remembered his first crush and his father talking to him just like this. He tried to think of the things he was sorry his father hadn't said. After a moment he continued,

"Well, Grayson. If you don't want her to forget you, then give her something to remember you by. That's all I can say."

He patted Grayson on the back, and they both returned to work.

A day or so passed. No lessons, but Oh'Dar did lots of work in the stables and fields. He gave a great deal of thought to Mr. Jenkins' advice. What could he give Miss Blain that would make her remember him in the way he wanted?

Finally, the day came. Miss Blain had her lesson materials and her personal items packed and ready to go, and the bags were loaded onto the carriage. She was about to leave but hadn't forgotten her promise. She walked toward the stables to find Oh'Dar and say goodbye.

Mr. Jenkins saw Miss Blain coming and went out to meet her to make sure to say his goodbyes first. He thanked her for the fine job she did with Grayson and said he hoped they might see her again someday. Before he was done, Oh'Dar showed up, so Jenkins stepped back to give them some privacy.

"Master Grayson, all my things are loaded, and I'm ready to leave. I promised you I wouldn't go without saying goodbye. I'm sure your new teacher will be just what you need to get you ready for your next step. It has been a pleasure to teach you, and I'm confident you'll do well in whatever you choose."

You're being so formal with me? Let's see how formal holds up after this.

"The pleasure has been all mine, Josephine." He whispered her first name and at the same moment, quickly swept her into his arms, leaned her backward and kissed her long and hard.

When he released her, she almost fell over, so he grabbed her and pulled her back to him again. As once before, long ago, she was in his arms looking up into those blue eyes. Because she hadn't struggled free, he kissed her hard again and *then* set her upright on her feet.

With that, he tipped his hat, turned, and walked back to the stables, leaving her standing there trying to regain both her balance and her composure. Her face was flushed and her hair mussed.

As he walked away, he shouted back to her without turning around, "I hope you'll remember me, Miss Blain."

Catching her breath, and knowing he was out of earshot, she replied, "It will be impossible not to, Master Grayson."

Standing a little distance away watching the whole thing, Mr. Jenkins was about to bust a rib trying not to laugh. As Oh'Dar walked jauntily over to him, a little attitude in his step, Mr. Jenkins slapped him on the back.

"Damn, son. You sure do know how to leave an impression. She'll be thinking about that kiss for weeks," he laughed.

"Well, you told me to give her something to remember me by," he said, grinning from ear to ear.

"I was thinking of a letter or a pretty flower, Grayson. But I have to say I like your idea much better!"

They both smiled and got back to work.

Oh'Dar was happy to have Mr. Jenkins around. He was like a friend, a brother, an uncle, and maybe even a father. Every day the young man looked forward to helping the stable master. Oh'Dar was ready to start his lessons again, but he very much doubted his new teacher could be as pretty as Miss Blain.

From the porch swing, Miss Vivian saw the whole thing. She chuckled to herself.

You have to hand it to that boy; on top of everything else he's got nerve!

She couldn't fault him, but found she felt sorry for Miss Blain now—being kissed like that and then turned loose! *Gracious.*

He's got his father's charm too. Oh, he's going to break a lot of hearts, she thought to herself.

CHAPTER 10

K hon'Tor was up early—for some reason thinking about those who had come forward requesting to be paired. There was Akule who had come to him a while back, and some of the females in the community who would be coming of age by the time the High Council made their decisions. As for himself, there had not been any opportunity to see who the available females from the other communities might be. He would have to hope that he would be able to select someone in the days before the announcement.

In the past, he had been drawn to high spirited females like Adia. He now knew how much he needed the sense of conquest to enjoy mating but was hesitant to select another fiery female. As much as he did not like the idea, he might have to choose one more mild-natured, whom he could intimidate into submitting to his particular ministrations.

Kthama was the only place large enough to host such a gathering. It was a great deal of work as there were sleeping quarters to prepare, extra meals, greeters to appoint, and many other logistics to consider. Luckily, he reflected, Acaraho was a master at organizing.

Acaraho and Khon'Tor met that morning to discuss the High Council meeting. It was customary for all the communities requesting pairings to let the High Council know how many would be coming, so there was enough time to plan. Those close to the Mother Stream would follow it underground to reach Kthama. Those who could not would travel only at night. Once Acaraho knew from which directions they would be coming, he would post extra watchers along their routes. The added factor of Waschini riders in the area required an additional level of security.

After they were done talking about the planning, Acaraho brought up the question of Nootau. "I want to let you know that Nootau will be requesting a pairing."

"That brings the total so far to four. Not as many as I would have thought," was Khon'Tor's bland reaction.

"Seeing that Nootau is your son, I thought you might be interested," is what Acaraho wanted to say but did not.

"I was hoping more of the young males would be ready. It would be good to have more offspring to keep our numbers high. But there are many coming up in the next few years after." Khon'Tor continued his indifference to Nootau.

Any females paired at the ceremony would be leaving the High Rocks. Newly paired males would bring new females into the community, increasing their numbers further as offspring arrived.

Khon'Tor was not going to come back to the topic of Nootau. "I hope we get candidates from some of the communities farther out. It has been a while since anyone from the Great Plains or High Red Rocks has participated. I know the journey is long and difficult, however."

Acaraho got up to leave. He noticed that Khon'Tor did not mention Oh'Dar, either. He had not shown any reaction when the boy left, which Acaraho found peculiar. It was coming up for a full cycle, and still Khon'Tor never asked about him. Considering how much commotion the boy's presence had caused, it seemed out of place. Acaraho thought he would test the waters before he left.

"In case you are wondering, we have heard nothing more from Oh'Dar. The last I knew was that he arrived safely at the Waschini village and appeared to be in friendly hands," Acaraho said. "It will be a year in the spring," he added.

Still no response; Khon'Tor did not even look up at Acaraho. The silence said it all.

Acaraho finally left. He had suspicions that something had triggered Oh'Dar's departure. He and

Adia both had. But Adia had made peace with it, and Acaraho was loathe to risk stirring up her feelings again.

What is Oh'Dar doing? Is he safe? Will we ever see him again? These questions rolled over in Acaraho's mind as he went to find Adia.

He looked for her everywhere and eventually found her outside. It was a brisk, cold, gray day, and Kweeuu came bounding up to greet him. What had started as a little ball of fur had grown into a hundred-and twenty-pound adult grey wolf.

Kweeuu jumped up at Acaraho, who immediately gave the command for down, and the wolf complied. It was no matter if he jumped up at Acaraho, but they wanted to discourage that behavior because he could easily knock down an offspring.

They had wondered if Kweeuu might someday leave, as he was now mature. Several months after Oh'Dar had left, the wolf finally stopped lying outside the workshop door. Even though Adia would take him inside the workshop to show him that his master was not there, it was where Oh'Dar had been last, and Kweeuu kept vigil there, waiting for his return. Adia finally asked Urilla Wuti how she could let Kweeuu know that Oh'Dar was safe but not likely to return. Urilla Wuti herself had made only the briefest and shallowest of Connections with the grey wolf. It worked, and that was when Kweeuu stopped waiting for Oh'Dar to return. But even after all this time, it was clear he still missed the boy.

Kweeuu did disappear for days, but always returned. Luckily no one in the community had objected to his presence, even though he was no longer the cute little cub who weaved in between their feet and begged for scraps.

Acaraho made sure Adia knew he was approaching and came up to put his arm around her waist. He wanted to pull her up against him and run his hands all over her, but he knew he could not. Though there was no one outside with them, there were still the guards and watchers. They had to be satisfied with their Dream World lovemating and keep their hands off each other as much as possible during the day.

"I told Khon'Tor to put Nootau in for consideration. I'll let Nootau know as soon as I see him," Acaraho told her. Adia wove her fingers in between his as they rested on her waist. Even that little bit of contact started his blood racing.

"I hope Nootau will be as lucky as I have been. Even though we are not paired," he said.

"It makes me sad, Acaraho, that we cannot claim our relationship. I know everyone believes you are Nootau's father, but I still wish I could claim you openly. She turned and looked up at him and added, "I wish we could be together."

"We are together, Saraste'," he replied, tightening his fingers around hers and squeezing her waist again.

"You know what I mean."

"Yes, I do. I know. I did not mean to make light of it," Acaraho added. "The upcoming pairings are stirring up feelings for both of us, I know."

After a moment of silence, Adia changed the subject. "I wish I knew where Oh'Dar was and what he was doing. No, I know he is still alright. But it is hard not even knowing where he is. Do you think he will ever come back to us?" she asked.

Acaraho did not want to go there, but there they were.

"It depends on how far away he is, and if he wants to," Acaraho answered.

"Do you think he does not *want* to come back? *Ever*?" her voice cracked.

Acaraho turned her to face him, putting a hand on each of her arms so he could look at her.

"Wanting to come back and feeling he can come back are two different things. Do I think he would want to return someday? Yes absolutely. But depending on why he left, he may not feel he can," By this time Acaraho so wished he had kept his mouth shut.

"If you know something I don't, you need to tell me now," Adia urged.

"No, I do not know anything. It's just a suspicion. You have felt the same way; we have talked about it. Yes, Oh'Dar had his sullen moments, and Honovi told us he was struggling with fitting in. But when he came back after last summer, and we set up his workshop, he seemed happy again. Like his old self when he was a little boy. Then suddenly he left, telling us not to come after him," said Acaraho. "A sudden change in behavior like that is usually brought on by something."

"If something happened, then someone must know about it," Adia answered.

"Adia, you told me you have peace about his leaving. Do you want to stir this up? And with Nootau taking a mate? I know the next year is going to be hard enough on you as it is." He touched the side of her face.

She broke her own rules and put her arms around him, laying her head against his chest, seeking comfort.

"I do not know. I mean, I do know Oh'Dar is fine. But, yes, it still bothers me that he would up and leave suddenly, when everything had turned around. Do I want to open myself to being upset again? Of course not. But I feel I need to know."

Acaraho pulled back to look at her and nodded slowly.

"Right. I will see what I can find out. I will be discreet, and if someone knows something, hopefully they will come forward. I would hate to see you upset again."

"I know. But if something bad happened to send Oh'Dar away, we need to know."

Kweeuu squeezed in between them, ready to go for his morning scraps, so they returned inside.

At the morning meal, Acaraho sat down next to Nootau. "I've told Khon'Tor that you want to be considered for pairing," he started.

Nootau looked up and smiled profusely.

"Understand, son; this does not necessarily mean that you will be paired. It depends on the young females who are available. They will not pair you with anyone from our community; that only happens when a couple has created a specific bond and requests it. The High Council looks at the records and carefully considers who they match together."

"What records?" asked Nootau.

Nadiwani spoke up, "You know the Keeping Stone that I started for you when you were born? And how we keep track of each day and make a different mark for important events? Well, it is similar to that. I do not know how they do it, but they look at who the parents and grandparents are, and as far back as possible. In that way, they keep the People strong and healthy."

"What if I do not like her?" Nootau pursed his lips.

"So far, everyone paired has gotten along just fine," she said.

"What about Khon'Tor and his mate? You said they did not seem even to like each other most of the time."

Adia stepped in to explain. "The Leader has the

right to choose his own mate. It has been like that for as long as anyone can remember."

"I am glad I do not get to choose. I am glad the High Council chooses for us. I would be afraid of making a mistake, as Khon'Tor did."

Acaraho and Adia could not help but look at each other. If Khon'Tor had claimed him, as the next Leader, Nootau would have had to choose his mate.

Well, that's one good thing about the situation, I guess, thought Adia.

Sometimes she felt bad that Nootau had been cheated out of his right to be the next Leader of the People of the High Rocks. Other times, like this, she thought it had worked out fine. All his life, Nootau had considered Acaraho to be his father. To find out now that it was Khon'Tor would be upsetting, to say the least.

And then there would have been the obvious question as he got older and learned about mating, *How did it come about*? It was evident that there was no love lost between Adia and Khon'Tor.

Those were questions she did not want to answer. For Nootau to know that his birth father was the great Khon'Tor, Leader of the largest Sasquatch community in the region was one thing. It was another to know that his birth father was Khon'Tor, only the second male in the history of the People to break Sacred Law and mate a female Without Her Consent.

Acaraho took an indirect approach to find out what might have triggered Oh'Dar's departure. He could have asked directly, but in this case he felt a less overt approach might produce better results. First he called for a meeting with his First Guard, Awan.

"Good morning, Commander. What can I do for you?"

"Sit down, please. I have something I need to ask of you. I would handle it myself, but I think you will be more effective than I would," Acaraho explained.

"You know that our son Oh'Dar left about a year ago. His mother and I have been bothered about the reason ever since. Just before he left, everything was going well. We had set up his workshop—I know you remember because you helped do it—and he was excited about his new projects. I know he was. So what happened to make him leave? We have no idea."

"And you want me to ask around quietly to see if anyone knows anything. I will see what I can find out, Commander. I promise I will be careful."

"I know you will, Awan. That is why I came to you. I appreciate your loyalty and your willingness to help. Especially considering that this is a personal matter," he added.

"It may be a personal matter, but it affects others as well. Many were upset that Oh'Dar left. People still ask why. I think others would appreciate knowing—if it is something that can be made public," remarked Awan.

The two parted ways, and Acaraho went back to the huge task of hosting the next pairing celebrations, the Ashwea Awhidi.

CHAPTER 11

Finally came the day the new teacher was to arrive. As before, a carriage pulled up in the circular driveway. As before, Oh'Dar was there with his grandmother and Mrs. Thomas.

He was anxious to see his new teacher. It would be nice if she were even half as pretty as Miss Blain. But no matter how pretty she was, no one was going to take Miss Blain's place—in his heart, or in his thoughts at night.

As the wagon stopped, Oh'Dar thought there had to be some mistake. The driver in the front was a man, but no young woman was sitting in the back. Instead, there was a middle-aged man with some type of facial hair that Oh'Dar had never seen before. He stood there unmoving, perplexed at who this person was, and where the teacher could be.

The man dismounted and came over to greet them while the driver offloaded his baggage.

"Good Morning. My name is Samuel Carter."

Mrs. Morgan introduced herself and the others, then thanked Mr. Carter for coming.

Mr. Carter bowed and then extended his hand to shake Oh'Dar's. Somewhere along the way, in addition to unintentionally teaching Oh'Dar to swear, Mr. Jenkins had given him a lesson in this ritual.

Mrs. Morgan explained to Mr. Carter that his baggage would be delivered to his room, that he was welcome to rest up, and that someone would call him for dinner. Afterward, the two of them would meet to discuss Master Grayson's lessons.

Mr. Carter bowed just slightly and followed Mrs. Thomas up the long steps to the house.

"Grandmother," Oh'Dar jogged over to her before she could leave.

"I know, Grayson. You're disappointed that Mr. Carter is a man. We knew you would be. But Miss Blain and I discussed it before she gave me recommendations for her replacement." She took his arm so he would be sure to be looking at her as she continued.

"Miss Blain was a great teacher. I hope that Mr. Carter will be as good. But you don't need the distraction of a pretty young woman right now. No one blames you for being attracted to her, Grayson. It is perfectly natural, and I don't want you to think you did anything wrong. But you must admit that sometimes it was hard to keep your mind on your studies with her around," she said gently.

Oh'Dar wasn't offended by what his grandmother was saying. He knew she was right, and he nodded.

"You have the rest of your life to find someone to love, Grayson. And with your good looks and personality, you'll have your pick of the young ladies. Right now, you need to learn all you can and prepare yourself for the next step. We all want the best for you; I hope you know that."

"I do, Grandmother. I do. I just hope she doesn't forget about me," he said.

"Well, Grayson, I saw how you said goodbye to Miss Blain. I think I can assure you that she won't be forgetting you any time soon."

Oh'Dar blushed. It was one thing for Mr. Jenkins to see him kiss Miss Blain, but it felt entirely different that his grandmother had.

"Go and enjoy the last free day you'll be having for a while. I'm sure your lessons with Mr. Carter will start tomorrow."

She watched him walk away. "Sometimes, he still seems more of a boy, and at other times he seems as if he's already a man," she said to Mrs. Thomas.

Several days stretched by before Acaraho heard back from Awan. But finally, the First Guard asked to talk to him, and they met discreetly.

"I have information for you, Commander. But

you're not going to like it," he said, suggesting that they might want to sit down.

Acaraho tensed at Awan's words.

"There was an incident a while before Oh'Dar left. He was in the eating area, apparently with Kweeuu. The cub had wandered away, and Oh'Dar followed to where Khon'Tor was talking about him."

Acaraho pushed his hands through his hair, waiting for the rest.

"They were talking about Oh'Dar, and Khon'Tor remarked that Oh'Dar probably had people somewhere who were still looking for him. And that Oh'Dar would bring disaster to the People. And something about if that happened it would be his mother's fault. By the look on his face, the boy overheard them," Awan explained.

"I am not going to ask who the other party was; it is enough to know that something made Oh'Dar decide to leave, as I suspected." Acaraho got up and walked about to clear his mind.

"Commander, are you going to confront Khon'Tor?"

"No, Awan, I am not. Nothing will be served by that except to get your source into trouble. We all know that Khon'Tor has periodically taken issue with Oh'Dar's presence. Thank you for your help."

Acaraho knew he had to tell Adia, but he dreaded it. She would know how Khon'Tor's words must have cut Oh'Dar to his soul.

Adia was with Nadiwani when Acaraho found

her. He seldom did so, but this time he asked Nadiwani if he could speak with Adia alone.

"You found something out about Oh'Dar?" she asked after Nadiwani had left.

"Yes. I hate to tell you this. But it is as we suspected, something did happen that probably drove him to leave." He sighed and told Adia what Awan had found out.

One. Two. Three. Acaraho readied himself to console her.

"Well, that's great news," she said.

A tiny white feather floating on the breeze could have knocked over the mighty Acaraho.

"*Tell me why this is great news*?" he asked gingerly, not wanting to break whatever spell had come over her.

"I had an experience while I was in the Connection with Urilla Wuti. I learned why I had to leave my home to become the Healer at Kthama. And in part, it had directly to do with Oh'Dar. Do you remember I told you that when I found him, I knew saving him was somehow going to be important to us all? Well, Khon'Tor is wrong. Oh'Dar came to help us, not to cause us difficulties. He is not going to bring disaster to us. Quite the contrary—

"This means Oh'Dar can come home. He only left because he was afraid that being here would cause problems. Once he knows that is not true, he will be free to come home." Her voice was filled with hope.

"I just have to let him know. That's why he left his bear. He left it to tell me he did not want to leave but felt he had to! Oh, Acaraho, I am so happy. Thank you so much!" Adia exclaimed.

Acaraho was relieved to see her reaction. And he was certainly not going to bring up the small problem of how in the world they would find Oh'Dar to tell him all this.

Oh'Dar had a chance to get to know a little more about Mr. Carter at dinner that night. He seemed quite proper—if that was the correct word. He was more formal than Miss Blain, and he didn't laugh as easily, but then he was a man, so that was to be expected.

All in all, Oh'Dar decided he would be able to get along with Mr. Carter. Maybe his grandmother was right. It would be easier to concentrate on his studies without the distraction of Miss Blain, even in her baggy Mrs. Thomas clothes.

By spring, Oh'Dar had come a long way. He had learned a great deal under Mr. Carter's instruction, and Mr. Carter said that Master Grayson would be ready to undergo specialized medical instruction sooner than expected.

Dr. Miller was more than happy to take Oh'Dar on as an apprentice. But since Oh'Dar had no experience at all, Dr. Miller preferred to wait until he had completed whatever specialized instruction was available. Based on the reports of both Mr. Carter and Dr. Miller, Mrs. Morgan started her search for a hospital that would provide such supplemental training.

Back at Kthama, spring brought an additional air of celebration as Khon'Tor called a general meeting about the upcoming pairing ceremony.

Everyone was seated as the Leader strode confidently to the front. As he always did, he raised his left hand before speaking, dropping it after everyone had quietened down.

"I will be brief, but I have a couple of announcements to share with you. The High Council will be gathering soon to review the pairing requests for the Ashwea Awhidi, next spring. If you wish to be considered for pairing and have not yet let me know, the time to do so is now. I do not know when the next opportunity will be. As you know, it has been some time since the last full-scale celebration. So far, we have twelve of our own who wish to be paired. Of course, we will be losing our young females to other communities, but we will also be gaining mates for our unpaired males."

Khon'Tor walked a few feet away from where he had started. Adia and Acaraho looked at each other; he only did this when he was changing the topic in some way.

"At the last meeting, Kachina was brave enough to ask me about my situation. It has been many years since I lost my mate, Hakani. I have not wanted to take another mate; however, I do need to produce an heir. I will not live forever, and I must put my responsibilities above my personal preferences. So, I intend to select another mate, and hopefully at this celebration."

Khon'Tor raised his hand to signal the end of the meeting.

"Thank you, that is all."

He left the front of the room amid a great deal of excited conversation. The eyes of nearly all the females followed him even more closely as he walked by, no doubt imagining what it would be like for the lucky young female who would be paired with the magnificent and virile Khon'Tor.

Adia and Acaraho had been standing against one of the rock walls, but Nadiwani and Nootau were sitting together with Mapiya, Haiwee, and Pakuna.

"I wonder who has asked to be paired," pondered Haiwee.

"I have asked," said Nootau.

They all congratulated him.

"Nootau, you are growing into a fine young male. You are going to be as strikingly handsome as

Acaraho. And let's hope that taking a mate will improve Khon'Tor's disposition. He has been so irritable lately," joked Mapiya.

"Well, it certainly cannot hurt!" said Nadiwani.

Hearing the laughter, Adia and Acaraho walked over and joined their makeshift extended family.

They took a spot next to each other. Even though they were not openly joined, Adia could not have asked for a better mate than Acaraho. Animated by the news that Oh'Dar had left based on a misunderstanding, she was in high spirits. She pressed her leg against Acaraho and entwined her feet around his. Making every effort to be discreet, she slipped her hand under the table and ran it purposefully up his thigh, threatening to make it impossible for him to leave the table for some time. Acaraho raised his eyebrows and gave her a warning look as if to say, *"Keep it up, female, and I'll clear this table and take you right here and now!"*

Of course he wouldn't. And since they had discovered a way to be together in the Dream World, they had relieved a great deal of pressure. Knowing they had a method of release, they enjoyed flirting and teasing each other. With no threat of seeding, it was the perfect solution. They had all the pleasure of being with each other, and to Adia's great joy, their convoluted relationship no longer denied Acaraho a male's satisfaction of mating. As Healer, Adia had abandoned the possibility of having a mate or offspring. Yet somehow, by the grace of the Great Mother, she had both.

Adia had thought long about what her father had told her in the Corridor; that there would be great struggles ahead and that she needed to bring herself into balance with all three of the gifts of the Great Spirit. Adia was known for her big heart, and it was her blessing to others. But her father's words had hit home. That was only one of the three aspects of the Great Spirit. There were also the Great Will and the Great Mind. Adia knew that her father's words contained profound knowledge and within his statements were innumerable gifts of insight and wisdom if she would invest the time to pursue them.

Brought out of her thoughts by the laughter, Adia glanced around the table and counted her blessings.

Soon Nootau will be paired and have offspring of his own. It is harder for Nadiwani to have him leave to establish his own family, as Nootau shares her quarters with him. But he will not be leaving the community as Oh'Dar did—he will just be moving out from under her roof. Watching him grow from a tiny offspring to the male he is becoming has been an amazing experience. And hopefully, not long after he is paired, there will be offspring to celebrate. So, all-in-all, my family is growing.

But in her heart, there would always be two empty places at the table, one for Oh'Dar and the other for Nimida, Nootau's sister. All she knew about Nimida was that she was healthy and well—the Connection Urilla Wuti had created between herself and her daughter gave her that much at least. But as to her whereabouts or the conditions of her life, Adia was not able to receive any information.

As for Oh'Dar's empty spot, at least she now had hope that he would return home. *Once he understands that he is not a threat to the People, there will be no need for him to stay away. Perhaps with Urilla Wuti's help, I could find out where he is and get a message to him. Oh, how I wish I knew what he is going through.*

Of course, Urilla Wuti could only tell her that he was healthy and adjusting to his new life. Any more than that, she would not share—Urilla Wuti was always concerned about interfering with fate and would reveal only the information necessary to ease Adia's mind.

The time between now and the Ashwea Awhidi would be a joyful one. Yes, there would be sadness as the newly paired females left their community. It was hard for families to give up their daughters. But it was necessary for the health of the People, and the First of the First Laws was clear. The needs of the community took precedence over the needs of any individual.

Adia was jolted out of her reverie by Acaraho's tantalizing revenge taking place under the table. It was her turn to give him an incredulous look. They both knew they would be turning in early that night!

Nootau was watching his parents, and though he did not know what precisely was going on between them, he knew their playful lovingness was what he wanted in his pairing.

All things considered, Adia had made it through every trial so far. Despite the hard times, the attack by Khon'Tor, her having to give up Nimida for her own good, Hakani's kidnapping of Nootau, and Oh'Dar's leaving, she not only had come out enriched by all of it—she had hope for the future. The currents of life would always bring challenges and blessings; she realized that now. And no matter how difficult a situation might be, the Great Spirit had a way of bringing good out of every hardship. No longer merely believing, but now knowing this to be true, a quiet peace entered Adia's heart.

Back in his Quarters, Khon'Tor sighed heavily, deep in thought. Announcing that he would be taking a new mate had stirred up his appetites. There was another year to go before the pairing ceremony.

Once I have her, I cannot exactly indulge myself immediately. I will have to work up to it over time. And I might have to wait until she produces the male heir I need, and her dependence on me is assured before I can bend her to my tastes.

Khon'Tor did not know if he could wait that long. He had allowed his thoughts to dwell on his attack on Adia, which had started him down this dark path. He began to consider how he might be able to meet his needs without exposure. And the more his plans began to gel, the more the tension within him started to build.

No, there was no way Khon'Tor was going to be able to wait that long.

/

PLEASE READ

I am humbled by your continued interest in my writing. If you enjoyed this book, I would very much appreciate your leaving a review or at least a rating.

Reviews give potential readers an idea of what to expect, and they also provide useful feedback for authors. The feedback you give me, whether positive or not so positive, helps me to work even harder to provide the content you want to read.

If you would like to be notified when the other books in this series are available, or if you would like to join the mailing list, please subscribe to my monthly newsletter at my website https://leighrobertsauthor.com/contact

Wrak-Ayya: The Age of Shadows is the first of three series in The Etera Chronicles. The next book in this series is: Book Four: *The Healer's Blade*

ACKNOWLEDGEMENTS

To you, who continues to honor me with your interest in my writing.

To my brother Richard who continues to be one of my staunchest supporters.

And to everyone else who put up with me through this.

I owe you.

A lot.

Made in the USA
Las Vegas, NV
25 September 2023

78139210R00166